MAGICAL PROBI

BOOK TWO IN THE FEDERAL WITCH SERIES

TS PAUL

GREAT GOD PAN PUBLISHING

Legal Stuff

Cover designed by Heather Hamilton-Senter

Edited by Laurie Holding

Formatted by Nina Morse

Special thanks to my wife Heather who keeps me grounded and to Merlin the Cat, we are his minions.

CHAPTER ONE

"CAT HAVE you seen my dress shoes?"

"Cat?" I pulled my head out from under the bed to see my diminutive roommate sound asleep at her desk. I stood up from beside the bed and crossed the room. Her head was down on one of her textbooks, drool pooling on the page. Smiling, I grabbed my cell phone from my pocket and took a candid shot. It was too good not to! Today was a very big day and if I didn't get to take a nap neither did she.

I gave her a shake and spoke into her ear. "Hey, get your ass up! Don't you want to graduate?"

She stirred a little, and I could hear a muffled voice. "Go away. I'm taking a power nap here."

"You can rest all you like when the ceremony is over. Now, get up."

"Don't wanna!"

"Don't make me call Chuck. He can get you up."

"Not if I order him not too."

"You won't do that. You like Chuck too much to mess with him like that." It was true. Chuck was part of our little gang here on campus. He was way too nice to screw around.

"Fine. Whatever." She raised her head off the desk and rubbed her face. "Eeeww nasty!" She wiped the drool off onto a towel by the desk.

I just laughed at her. I would save that picture for blackmail material. You never know when something like that can come in handy. Today was an important day; it was graduation day. The end of the third year was momentous for us wanna-be agents. For non-field agents this was it. The end of their Law Enforcement Training. Specialized training would now start. They would go on to become the power behind the muscle that makes up the Bureau; office staff, trainers, and lab technicians. The rest of us would partner with actual field agents and our last year was on-the-job-training intensified! Cat was scheduled to intern with the behavior analysis unit for her fourth year. The last time I spoke with Chuck, he was going to the forensic field unit. He was very excited. As yet no one had given me my assignment. With any luck, Director Mills will do that after the ceremony.

Checking the clock I told Cat she had thirty minutes to get ready. Living with the WereCat Alpha, I learned that she was perpetually late, so I always gave her short time limits. "Have you seen my shoes?"

"Look over by Fergus's barn. I saw him sleeping in one of them the other day."

"What? If that little maniac ruined my shoes, it'll be back to the shoebox for him!" I stepped over the small table we had set up near the window. His red barn was in the middle of the table, and sure enough, there were my shoes! My shoes were sitting neatly together and lined up perfectly so they could not be seen behind the barn.

"Fergus!" I opened the barn door to the sound of mooo from the noisemaker on the door. Peering inside there was no sign of him. I reached for one of my shoes, and I could see hay down in the bottom of it. I turned the shoe upside down, and I gave it a shake. Bits of hay and a startled Unicorn hit the top of my desk.

"I was sleeping!" He looked rattled, but nothing was broken. It takes a lot to break a Unicorn. Just ask Grams cat, Zeus. He bounces Fergus around like a toy ball.

"Fergus, why are you in my shoe?"

"I was camping."

"In my shoe?"

"It's my summer home."

"What? How did you even get them up here?"

"I jumped."

"Really? Did you jump carrying my shoes? I'll bet you got Chuck to put these up here for you."

Fergus just stared at me. "If you aren't going to, believe me. I'll just go home then." He walked around to the front of the toy barn and went through the door. The noisemaker made a Mooo sound.

Unicorns. I shook my head. Just when I think I understand him, he does something that makes me doubt myself. I sat on the bed and slipped my shoes on. I had to take them off again and clean out the hay. Summerhouse indeed.

"Cat are you ready yet?" I could see movement in the closet, but no tiny roommate had emerged yet.

"Tell me why we have to go to this thing again?"

"It's graduation. At least the schooling part. They did explain it to us. I know you heard it. We finished our three years of coursework and now we specialize for a year. On the job training is what Director Mills called it."

"I just want to go back to sleep."

"No sleeping for you Missy. Isn't your father here? I know my grandmother is."

"Both mom and dad are here. I'm just afraid to see them. I don't want them subservient to me because of my Alpha status."

"He's your father. Just keep telling your Cat that and it will be fine. Isn't this base considered neutral ground?"

"It is, I keep forgetting that it is. You're right. My parents came all this way just to see me graduate and take pictures. Come on let's go." Cat grabbed my arm and pulled me out of the room. We passed several of the other graduates and newer residents on our way out, and they all gave us a wide berth. The events of last year and the battle at Fabulous Face leaked to the other students as well as the press. Having most of an entire town be consumed by demons was news. It was almost impossible for the FBI to keep secret that we were involved in it. It just added to the mystique. Both Cat and I shrugged it off. Let them be afraid of us. We were leaving anyway.

The ceremony was taking place at the soccer field. It was the only place large enough with places for civilians to sit. There were more private areas over on the Marines side, but they weren't very happy with the FBI at the moment. That's not completely true. They were upset with me. Personally, I had a not so nice conversation with the director a couple of weeks ago over the whole thing.

"Agatha I have a bone to pick with you." The look on the director's face was not a good one. I tried to think about anything I may have done recently.

"Ma'am if this is about the landscaping on the East lawn I promise I will pay for it." The look she gave me froze me in place.

"No, this is about something else, but we will be discussing the East lawn. That explains the crying groundskeeper I had in here this morning. This is about these." She held up a picture.

It was all I could do but wince. The picture showed what looked like the Marine Barracks parade ground. It was covered in Jackalopes. The little critters had eaten all of the grass there.

"Oh, those. If you remember last year before you sent me after that Demon I mentioned those things. They were a tiny accident."

The director cocked her head to one side as if thinking. "I sort of remember that conversation. Help me to remember please?"

"I told you about the spell that went wrong during the last practice with the council's teacher, Montgomery something or other was his name. I made one of those but later saw a couple more. I did tell you about them."

"Nope doesn't ring-a-bell. These things..."

"Jackalopes." I smiled at her.

She frowned at me. "As I said, these... Jackalopes have infested the entire forest and the Marine base. I just had the General on the phone screaming at me about them. He just knew it was you. His magical corporate goons told him you were the one that did it. He also said it was illegal and against the Council's magical laws?"

"Tampering with animals or people on purpose is against the rules. Accidents, however are not. Especially if you can prove that it was an accident. The Council is aware of the Jacks. Both grandmother and I informed them. I am sorry I didn't follow up after the demon thing. To be truthful, I forgot about them."

"This is a big deal, Agatha! The Marines are really pissed."

I squeezed my eyes shut and said a prayer to the goddess for strength. "I can try to zap them but every time I have changed an animal I made it magic proof. The squirrels and Fergus are proof of that. Do you want me to try?"

"Lord no. You might make them giants or something. I suppose we can call in hunters or exterminators."

That gave me an idea. "Ma'am what if we allow the Were's on campus to have a hunt? We can call it the annual Jackalope hunt or something."

Director Mills just gave me that look that made me think of kindergarten children. "I better not find out this was a gimmick to let your pack go hunting here. I will look into it."

Thus the semi-annual Jackalope hunt was born. The Were's loved it. Rabbits that fight back? They were in. Lots of contests and barbecue's that weekend. The administration might call it the Jackalope hunt, but the Were's called it the Jack-Off hunt. Some things I will never live down.

I could hear the crowd as we approached. We were supposed to gather at the home team side of the field. The Academy provided flimsy caps and gowns. Many of the other students said it was like High School. Never having been to one of those I had no idea. Cat and I slipped the plastic gowns on over our clothes and grabbed a hat. It was kind of hokey to do this, but I could see the benefit. We would be moving on to our specialties and would have little time to come back here to have one of these. Better to have it now. I peered at the crowd in the stands. I had not seen Grams in three years. I could use a friendly face.

The Director's assistants, the B's, seemed to be in charge out here. They managed to get the lot of us lined up into order. No names would be called. We either graduated or we didn't. We would march out, bow and be presented our diploma. A few speeches and we could break to find our families. Or at least that was what we were told. Hopefully the speeches wouldn't be long.

The crowd quieted as the Director stepped up to the podium. She had a nice speaking voice as she began to talk of the code of justice and what graduation meant for all of us. At a prearranged signal we marched out onto the field and stood at the Director's back as she wrapped up her speech. To this day I can't be sure what triggered it. It may have been an unsanctioned Were hunt or Mother Nature giving us the finger, but it was a disaster.

There we stood all in a line about to be awarded our diplomas when a herd or flock of Jackalopes entered the picture. Over fifty of the little buggers came loping through the ceremony. They got confused by all the people and scattered into the crowd and everything. Caps and gowns went flying as we tried to get away from the little horned devils. All I could do was stand there with my hands over my face. Cat who stood beside me began to laugh so hard she fell to the ground. Director Mills stared at the running animals and shrieking family members. She slowly turned and stared at me. I smiled and gave her a little wave. I was in big trouble.

CHAPTER TWO

THE LECTURE WAS NOT AS bad as it could have been. There were too many VIPs and parents on campus for Director Mills to rip me a new one over the Jackalope thing. She wasn't happy with me. All the good will I had built up with her seemed to vanish overnight because of the Jacks. The graduation procession may have been ruined, but it would be a very memorable graduation in all of our minds. I was helping set chairs aright when I spotted Grams sitting at the back of the parent's section. I yelled and waved at her.

Grams gave a big hug. She pulled back from me. "Let me look at you, child." She nodded her head. "You look more and more like my mother at that age. Remind me to send you some pictures. You've grown."

"You think so?" I looked down at myself. "I don't see it."

"You have filled out a bit and gained maybe an inch on top. You won't really notice it in your clothes." She looked at me sternly. "I assume those were your's?"

"The Jackalopes? Yeah. I told you about those, remember? That spell that Montgomery had me do. I did inform the Council about them."

"I did as well. You have to be careful Agatha. These and the squirrels were accidents, but someday you may do this on purpose and have to face the consequences. If that happens, I cannot protect you. You choices will be very slim. Be careful, child."

I nodded my agreement and took her warning to heart. "Now introduce me to these friends of yours. The day's a wasting."

Taking her hand, I led my grandmother over to where my roommate was.

Cat's father was a large man dressed in a business suit. His resemblance to one of my favorite movie stars was striking. I threw a quick glance at Cat. The little stinker purposefully did this to me. She had never once shown me a picture of her father, so I was surprised when he introduced himself. Part of me wanted him to lift me up and tell me I was flying.

"You must be Agatha, nice to meet you at last." Cat's blond father bent and kissed my hand making me blush. He turned toward Grams and bowed. "Milady Blackthorn."

Startled by what he called Grams I glanced at her. My grandmother had a mischievous glint in her eye as she inclined her head to the Were. "Consul, it's been a few years."

"That indeed it has Milady. From what I have learned you raised a good one in her." He was looking in my direction.

"She takes after her mother, and yes I have great expectations for Agatha. She will do great things."

"With luck, so will my daughter. They are a team, are they not?"

Grandmother nodded to the Were. Both Cat and I were staring at them. There was some sort of conversation going on between them that we just didn't understand. I looked at Grams and asked. "Um, grandmother do you know Mr. Moore?"

"We have met before. It was a great many years ago. One day we will talk about how I know of him but today is not the time." She glanced at her watch. "Are we not supposed to be at some sort of social or something?"

"Yes, Ma'am. We are. Director Mills has a social gathering set up for the parents and guardians in the main hall; we can show you the way."

"Let us be off then." She gestured toward the main building. I guessed the previous discussion was now over.

"Agatha, about those creatures, the Jackalopes?" I looked at Cat's dad.

"Yes, Sir?"

"You created them?"

"Yes, it was sort of an accident. The Council knows all about it, so I'm not in trouble with them. The administration around here aren't very happy with me, however. I forgot to follow up with them. Well, you saw what happened."

"I did indeed. Cat mentioned something about a hunt?"

"I suggested that the Were's here on campus be allowed to hunt them to reduce the population. Around here it's working, not so sure about the rest of the base."

"Are they edible?"

"Oh, yeah. Chuck and his buddies have been having barbecue cook-offs with the ones they catch. The Were's love them! They say that catching them is a challenge. Rabbits that fight back."

"Interesting. Cat? Could you have your classmates catch a few breeding pairs for me? I think they would make a good addition to the reserve back home."

"Dad, are you sure? They breed like crazy."

"We can control them. Your brothers and the others need some challenges."

"Sure, I guess. I'll give Chuck a call and see what we can do. You will have to pay for the cages."

"Money is not an issue. Tell your friends I will pay them a hundred dollars a pair as an incentive. They must be alive and in good condition." Mr. Moore motioned with his hands and made pointing directions as he talked.

"I'll call him right now. Chuck needs the money for car repairs." She whipped out her cell phone and began dialing. Chuck answered almost immediately. He had been at graduation but returned to the dorm. His parents didn't come to the Academy. Politics got in the way. He was no longer Pack to them and even though this was neutral ground, it was an issue with his enforcer brothers. I could tell from the way Cat nodded her head that Chuck was all in for the capture and cage. I could almost feel his approval of the task through the pack bonds we had created this year. The spell I used was supposed to build with time. It was still too new to be completely sure. I shrugged it off. We were approaching the main cafeteria, and I needed to be alert.

There was a small line to get inside, so I had just a minute alone with Grandmother. "How is the family? Camilla still causing trouble?"

"At the moment, no. Her brood, on the other hand, has always been trouble. Winter and Autumn have been caught tourist tipping a few times. Poor Cappy is at his wit's end over those two."

I smirked. Winter was my age and should know better. Autumn was the younger of the two. Whatever possessed my aunt to name them after seasons is the real question. "Was anyone hurt?"

"Not yet, fortunately. Those two have done more harm than you ever did. The squirrels hate them by-the-way. I have seen them go out of their way to drop nuts and excrement on them." She peered at me closely. "You don't have anything to do with that do you?"

I really couldn't hide very much from her. "I sort of asked them to chase Camilla when I was nine. She said something nasty to me, and I was upset. It was the only time they have ever listened to me, I swear. If they are chasing the girls, it is all on them!"

Grandmother began to laugh. "You. You are the reason they flock to her yard and throw nuts at her. Dear, I wish you had told me that years ago! We brought in animal experts to try and get them to stop." She chuckled some more and shook her head. "Your aunt has been saying you set them on her for years and no one believed her. Do not tell anyone else this. We shall keep this our secret. Understood?"

I nodded to her. The line began to advance. Director Mills stood at the front of the line welcoming each guest in personally. "Hello again, Agatha. Is this your Grandmother?"

"Yes, Ma'am. This is my grandmother Marcella Blackmore."

The Director took my grandmother's hand. "Your granddaughter has become a valuable asset to us here at the Bureau. Thank you for bringing her to us."

"Thank you for getting rid of your predecessor. But you're welcome. So far you have done a good job with her, she still respects her elders and is polite. Between you and me, I kicked the Council in their posterior and made them send competent instructors for her."

"Um, Grams?" I'm guessing she didn't know about the instructors.

Grandmother held her hand up to me to silence me. Knowing her like I did I shut my mouth.

"I'm sorry you went to that trouble, Mrs. Blackmore. The Council decided not to send any more instructors for Agatha this year. She was forced to learn on her own the spells that were needed. They sent written instructions along with spell books."

Grandmother turned toward me in shock. "What? Child, you should have contacted me!"

"Grandmother, I thought you knew. The instructions were fairly easy to do. I think I have a handle on it now."

She shook her head. "Those idiots! You will have to show me the instructions at your lab. I will be speaking to them about their idea of instruction, very soon. Maybe they will survive it."

Director Mills looked a bit alarmed by grandmother's outburst and stuttered a reply. "Mrs... Blackmore. Don't cause the FBI any trouble over this, please? We need a good relationship with the Witches Council."

Grandmother smiled at the director, and I cringed. It was the same 'Go to Hell' smile she used with Camilla.

"Don't worry Director Mills; they will respect you when I'm done with them." She was rubbing her hands together as if planning something. This was not good.

"Marcella are you causing the good Director here trouble?" Cat's father pushed his way past me and shook the Director's hand. His appearance broke through the gloom that had descended upon us all. "Robert Moore, nice to meet you."

"You must be Catherine's father. Nice to meet you at last. Did you know she is the first female Alpha at the Academy?"

"Actually I didn't know that." He moved in closer to the Director and began to talk to her about the Jackalopes and other Were issues. I glanced at Cat and smiled. That was very timely of her father to break in like that. Grandmother was about to set something on fire. I looked back at her, and she was just staring at the good looking Were.

I stepped over and touched her arm. "Are you alright?"

She looked at me and smiled. "Of course child. I'm fine. Let's go in and socialize a bit. I need to eat something and relax for a moment. We can talk later when you show me your laboratory." I smiled and led her into the cafeteria. Several dozen parents and students were wandering around. Tables were set up with finger food and snacks. I sat grandmother down at one of the empty tables and went up to the food line. Many of the staff were on duty serving, and I was able to chat with them. They all congratulated me on my graduation. My Winters of living here were almost over.

Walking back to the table, I found Cat and her father sitting and talking to grandmother. Cat's father was doing most of the talking. "... Marcella, please don't do anything rash. They are the devil we know. Replacing them could be worse."

"You have a point Robert, but I will still bring my displeasure to them. They should know by now not to cross my family or me. I will take your advice under advisement." She looked up into my eyes. "Ah, Agatha. Is that for me?"

"Uh, what?" I had been trying to understand their conversation and lost track of my own.

"The plate dear?" I looked down at my hands and blushed. Gods what an idiot I was today!

"Sorry," I handed it to her and sat down next to her at the table. "So how do you two know each other?"

Grandmother looked at Robert and gave him a smile. Looking back at me she replied. "Socially, dear. Robert and I share some mutual acquaintances. I will tell you about it someday. Let's just say we know each other and leave it at that shall we?" Look she gave me was not one that I would cross so I left it alone. Grandmother has many secrets.

I LOOKED at Robert and caught his eye. "Did you want so see my lab along with grandmother? It's not on the official tour, but Cat and I spend a lot of time there."

Glancing at my grandmother, he looked back at me and smiled. "Not this trip Miss Blackmore. Cat will fill me in on anything she thinks I should know. I have transportation to organize and I need to find some cages. If you ladies will excuse us?" He stood up from the table and motioned to Cat to follow him. I watched my roommate leave then looked back at Grams.

"So, want to see the lab now?"

"Of course I would. Is it very far?"

"It's a few miles away, but the Director let me borrow one of the grounds keeper carts for this event. Usually, I get Chuck to take me out there or just hike. Cross-country it's not too far." I stood up and pointed toward the kitchen. "It's parked in the rear out of the way. We can cut through here."

The kitchen staff were all present and said their hello's as we cut through the kitchen. I introduced Grandmother along the way to some of my favorite staff as we walked. These were the people that fed me and asked after me on a daily basis. Grandmother actually complimented the chef on his appetizers and they exchanged recipes for a few minutes. I smiled at my friends as I led her out the back door.

"Those are some very loyal people Agatha; they really care about you."

"They have been there for me during the winter breaks. I just did what you always told me to do."

"What was that dear?"

"Kill them with kindness. When I first got here quite a few on the staff were frightened of me after the incident with the former Director. I tried to be polite and friendly with everyone, and most of them came around eventually. Most of the staff now barely blink when I enter the room. The students, on the other hand, make up all sorts of stories about me. I ignore most of them." I led grandmother past the staff cars over to a four-wheeled cart at the edge of the lot. "Here we are. Hop on."

I pulled out the keys and fired the cart up. It was faster than a golf cart but not by all that much. I headed off toward the edge of the reserve telling grandmother about what I knew of the forest. I had to swerve a few times to avoid the Jackalopes. They were more of a problem on the Marine base than on our campus.

As we finally approached the gate to my lab grandmother remarked at the apparent security that I had.

"I like the fence you have. Did you have much trouble extending the wards out this far?"

"Not really. One of the Council teachers taught me how to do that. Of course, that was before I turned his beard bright red. That one really wasn't my fault. I did tell him my aim wasn't perfect." Grandmother smirked at me.

"Child, I heard some of the stories that the fools they sent tell about you and your magic. If I was to believe them, you are the worst witch since the one that house fell on. Can you believe they actually claim you conjured up a troll and it attacked the instructor?"

"Um, that one is sort of true."

Grandmother turned in her seat and stared at me. "Is it really?"

"Mostly. The instructor was Brady something. There have been so many of them that I forget the names. It was snowing, so we used one of the practice fields. It was near the highway, and he told me to use a 'detect creature' spell. I had never seen that spell before and told him that. He insisted that I do the spell, so I did an off-the-cuff one."

Grandmother shaded her eyes with her hand. "What happened?"

"It detected creatures all right. I had no idea there was a Frost Troll under that bridge! My spell located it and woke it up. It was quite mad. Like a bull, it took one look at Brady's red hair and took off after him. That was the last I saw of him. Hopping across campus with a large hairy troll in pursuit."

"Oh, dear. Maybe I should not have yelled at them so coarsely."

I smiled and triggered the spell on the gate. They unlocked and opened slowly. I related the story of the gate and how military intelligence wanted inside my lab.

"Serves them right. It's good you caught them. The explosion my trap would cause may have harmed them."

"Yes, I did try to tell the General that. They may try again soon. That reminds me, I do have something to show you."

We passed through the gates, and I closed and locked them behind me. Better safe than sorry. I parked the cart in front of the loading dock and led grandmother through the door.

"This is the main storage area." I pointed at the boxes piled around the room. "I have been making the magical bombs as you taught me. I pack and store them when completed. Thank you for teaching me how, they saved my life last year against that Demon."

"Agatha you are the future and the only grandchild that matters. Your cousins couldn't figure out how to make anything without blowing themselves up. Your Aunt has messed them up so badly."

"I remember how Winter acts. Is Autumn as bad too?"

"She's worse. That boarding school they sent her too gave her too many bad habits."

"That is one thing I've learned here. Bad habits lead to worse habits. Better to break them early. The greenhouse is through that door."

I opened the door to the lush jungle I had grown here. The long-neglected commercial greenhouse had become a witches paradise of magical herbology.

"Agatha this is why I call you the future! You grew all of this in three short years without any outside help. What do you have going on over there?" She pointed at the domed bed of grass.

"That is for Fergus. I cross-bred a couple species of hay to make a special blend. I use it as a reward. He gets to come and spend time rolling around in it."

"Really? Do you have seeds for me?"

"Of course I do." I reached into a small refrigerator and pulled out a small bundle of envelopes. "I have the hay here along with some local flowers and other herbs I've not seen at home. I thought your garden might enjoy them."

She took the packets and smiled at me. I led her back through the storeroom into my laboratory and office area. We sat at my desk to talk.

"Grandmother, what do you know about the bracelet?" I showed her the armband on my wrist.

"It took to you. Excellent. You are the first in two generations to wear it."

"What does it do?"

"When did you put it on?"

"Cat and I were at the FBI Critical Incident Response base camp for the kidnapping investigation we were assigned to. The agents were fighting amongst themselves to gain access to our equipment that was locked up. The Russian Mercs wanted my supplies, and I warded the car to prevent them from getting anything. I remember pulling it out of my pocket and slipping it on as I thought about what I wanted to do with my life. It tingled when the hasp clicked shut."

"It's a justice bracelet. They were used by the Enforcers of old to enhance the strengths of those that wore them. That one has been passed through the family for over two-hundred years. My grandmother was the last one to wear it. She told me it gave her a boost and talked to her sometimes."

"It talks?"

"I can only repeat what she told me. I was about ten at the time. I always hoped it would accept me."

"What happened to your grandmother?"

"Her name was Verity; it means truth in old English. She was a European Council Enforcer and one of the first to come to the new world. When I knew her, she was in retirement and very ancient. Women in our family live a long, long time Agatha. She had a very forceful personality. After her death, the bracelet passed into the possession of the head of the family. More than once the Council here in the new world has sought it out. It will protect you. Never allow anyone to remove it."

"Can it be removed?"

"I really don't know. Don't try, please."

"I won't, I promise."

"Good. Now, I know we discussed this on the phone, but I want you to tell me about the demon you stopped. All of it, please. It's very important that I know in case the Council brings it up to me as head of the family."

"OK." I then proceeded to describe the investigation and how we stopped the Demon from killing more people. It took about an hour to get through the entire story.

On the ride back to campus Grandmother took my hand. "Trust in yourself Agatha. Great power comes with great responsibility. You have to have faith."

I gave her a funny look. "Grams that was a line from that movie you took me to a few years ago, remember?"

"Was it? I'd forgotten." I could only smile at her. She has never forgotten anything in her whole life.

Her car was in the main parking lot waiting for her when we arrived. Like when I was a child the car looked the same with the chauffeur standing by to drive her.

"He hasn't been here the whole time has he?"

"No, he went into town to wait. I called him on my phone."She held up a cell phone.

"Grandmother is has been wonderful having you here."

She gave me a hug. "Agatha dear it was my pleasure to come. Now off you go. Finish your studies and reach your goal in life. Remember to trust yourself." We said our final goodbyes, and I watched as she drove away. I started to walk off the parking lot when I spotted Chuck and some of his friends. They were loading cages onto a storage van. I gave him a wave and called out his name.

"Hey, Aggy! We caught some!" I peeked into the truck and could see about a dozen very angry Jackalopes in cages. They were pawing at the cage mesh and trying to ram through with their horns.

"Did you get both males and females?"

"We did. Catching them live was a real challenge. I can fix my car now!"

"That's great Chuck. What about your friends?"

"I've got that covered. There is enough money to fix the car and have a big party. Not all the Jack's survived the hunt, so we're having a big barbecue tonight!"

I had to laugh. Chuck had a real thing for smoke and fire. I was surprised he didn't become a firefighter instead of a Government agent.

"I'll catch you later grill master. I need to go catch Director Mills before she leaves for the day." I jogged off the parking lot and headed toward the admin building. I still had not received my fourth-year assignment.

The blond receptionist wasn't in her bunker as I entered the building. It must have been her day off. It was too bad; I had a fresh insult all ready for her. After the problems of previous years, we actually had some detente going on. Our relationship had devolved to giving each other creative insults whenever we saw each other. It was fun.

I knocked on the door and heard "Come."

"Director?" I peered into her office.

"Agatha? Did your grandmother enjoy the tour?"

"She did. It gave us time to have a nice talk. She enjoyed herself."

"Excellent. Hopefully, she tells the Witches Council how well we have been treating you. Now, what can I do for you?"

"I haven't gotten my assignment for the fourth year yet. I thought I would ask you about it?"

"They didn't tell you? I know I made the memo." She scrabbled on her desk for a moment. "I'm sorry Agatha. It's right here. I must have missed giving it to the B's. Normally we would send you to a pool of new agents to train with for whatever assignment comes up but given your skill-set we are jumping the line so to speak. The Bureau has a Magical Crimes investigator that troubleshoots anything that comes up. We are assigning you to him for the year. He will be your new partner Probationary Agent Blackmore."

"What? Are you making me a Probi? This soon?"

"As I said. You are a special case. Normally he works with the hired help. But he will teach you what you need to know about investigative work and how your magic can help. He's a mundane but the best we have for this sort of thing. There are big plans at work with the higher-ups in relation to you and your abilities. All I know is they want you assigned to Magical Crimes for your fourth-year internship."

"Wow. OK. When do I meet the Agent-in-charge?"

"The last message I had was he was on his way. You should expect him sometime this week, I think."

"Thanks Director."

"You're welcome, Agatha. Hopefully, you learn what you need to know." She smiled at me as I left her office. I practically ran to the dorm. Just wait until I tell Cat and Chuck!

CHAPTER THREE

Chuck's massive beer and barbecue extravaganza got a bit out of hand, and the Marine MP's showed up when the music could be heard across the campus. Both Cat and I missed most of that excitement. We ate our Jack sandwiches, and each took a beer up to our room. My question is this how can people drink this stuff? I can't legally buy it but does it always taste so bad?

"Yuck!" It was all I could do to swallow my mouthful of beer. Cat sat on her bed with a beer in her hand laughing at me.

"The look on your face! Haven't you had alcohol before?"

"I've had wine and mead before. They are a sacrament in our solstice ceremonies. None of them tasted this bad!" I was smacking my lips trying to get the taste off my tongue. "How can you drink that?" She took another sip while I watched.

"It tastes pretty bad to me too, but my brother once told me that if you wanted to like something you needed to drink or eat it a lot to acquire the taste."

"Well, stop, please. It's making me sick just thinking about it. Besides, I know you want a clear head tomorrow for your new assignment."

"I do, thanks." She set the beer down and took a sip of her soda. "I'm jealous of you."

"Me? Why?"

"You get to leave and go off on a special internship. The rest of us have to wait until someone needs help. It will get boring around here without you Aggy."

"I'm sorry you can't come with me Cat, I really am. This whole thing is a surprise to me too. The Director told me this guy coming is special. He's the one that goes to all the magical crimes and tries to solve what the regular agents can't. I didn't even know we had a Magical Crimes division."

"Yeah, Chuck told me he saw it on the Division list, but thought they dissolved it years ago. I can't see how a mundane is able to solve anything, though."

"He could be from a magical family. That happens sometimes. I have at least one cousin who never showed any trace of powers. Last I heard he was a dentist in Portland. He stopped coming to the gathers."

"That's sad. It happens in Weres too. It's pretty rare for it to happen to Cats but the Wolves have that problem."

"They do? That wasn't discussed in class!"

"It's not a secret, but nobody likes to mention it. It only happens when we mate outside the species. I have a classmate from elementary school who mated with a regular human. He just had a few kits. None of them were human, but the whole clan was holding its breath."

"Could they have problems later?"

"Only if they mate with humans. Then their children might not shift. My community still accepts them, though. We don't exile someone because of who their parents loved."

"Has that happened?"

"It has. Dad told me about the last time. It was very messy. It makes me glad that I won't have a traditional pack or clan because I'm FBI. A few is all I want to deal with right now."

"You never know Cat, you might want to settle down with a mate one day?"

Cat gave me a funny look. "Settle down? Are you nuts? You and I are going places!"

I laughed at her expression. "You bet we are. Do you want to help me pack up tonight or tomorrow?"

"Tomorrow of course. Tonight we are watching movies and hanging out. I'm so going to miss you, Aggy." Cat stood and came over to give me a hug.

"Cat, we are friends and pack together. I will always be able to feel you. I'm just a phone call away. Feel free to call, OK?"

She nodded and began to pull movies off the shelf making a small pile.

"We are watching all those?"

"Maybe?"

"Let me pop some popcorn then." I stepped over to the microwave and fiddled with the controls. I heard Fergus come out of his house. "Mooo."

"Hey, Fergus. What's up?"

"I heard the word popcorn. You're making me some right?"

"No. This is for Cat and I. You have hay, I put some fresh in your stall not an hour ago."

"Maybe I want some popcorn instead?"

I shook my head. Unicorns. "What have you done to deserve it lately?"

"I've been good."

I looked at his mournful face. "Fine. You can have some. Are you ready for the new assignment?"

"What new assignment?"

"We talked about this. We leave tomorrow for our new assignment."

"Where are we going, and how do we get there?"

"No idea. Doesn't it sound fun?"

"No." He turned and went back into his barn.

I looked over at Cat and shrugged my shoulders. She just shook her head at me. The corn finished popping so I put a handful outside Fergus's door.

We spent the evening and most of the night watching chick-flicks and laughing.

MORNING CAME FAR TOO EARLY for my taste. It wasn't that I was hung-over, but when you go to sleep at four and get up at six-thirty, it can be a shock to the system. I hoped I would get a chance for a nap sometime today. I knew a small stay awake cantrip spell that Grandmother taught me, so I included it in my morning ritual. I honor the Gods as part of my daily observances. I say a prayer to start the day off right almost every morning if I am able. It is how I honor the traditions I was raised in. Ever since my meeting with Hecate last year I have felt closer to the Divine spirit. It gave me funny chills sometimes.

I started the job of packing up my clothing and spell supplies for my internship. I assumed that I would be able to come back from time to time to gather more supplies, so I had set the automatic watering systems at my lab yesterday. I hoped that the warning notices the military placed around my lab would keep out trespassers. I would hate to make a special trip back here to release an idiot who got too close.

Breakfast this morning was very subdued. Most of our class was still in bed somewhere. We sat down at our usual table and Jacob, one of Chuck's buddies sat down with us.

"It's a good thing you two left when you did."

"Why, what happened?"

"We got raided by the MP's and campus security. One of the junior's thought it was a good idea to put a live Jack inside the MP's Humvee."

Cat giggled and covered her mouth. "What idiot did that?"

"I don't know his real name. We all call him Mongo."

I smiled. "I've met him. One of the Werebears? He's this big goofy guy; he was in my shooting class. He might be a bit slow, but he's a master when he has a rifle in his hands."

"Right. He's the guy. They caught him, and he spilled about the party. Fortunately for us, we were out of beer when they showed up. They wrote us up on intoxicated in public and open containers. They were all empties, so they just have the drunk charges. Campus security told us not to worry too much about that. Those MP's don't have jurisdiction here on campus. They are still pissed about the Jacks."

"Yeah, the Director told me the Marines were unhappy."

"They may not like them, but we sure do! Free meat!"

I shook my head. Guys. "They were an accident."

"Sure they were. We know better." He laughed as he stood up. Giving us a wave he wandered over to another table.

I looked at Cat. "Do they really think I made those critters on purpose?"

Cat turned and looked at Jacob. "They do. Before you get upset, remember they don't know much about Witches. Nobody does. The clans and packs don't have very much contact outside of the reservations with other paranormals. You all are a big mystery to many of us. Dad has told us much about the others, and my uncle has a wizard on the payroll. But that is a rarity. Most of these others only know stories or bad things that happened to a pack member. Remember the looks you got the first year?"

I thought back to the some of the trouble I had over the past couple of years. I slowly nodded my head. "OK, I can see what you mean. But the magical community isn't that scary, at least not anymore."

"Agatha you forget that the only way most Weres come in contact with your kind is through investigations or those Russian guys. They don't know any better. Forget about them. You can't please all of the people all of the time."

We finished eating and put all our dishes in the dish station. I considered walking over to the Admin building, but figured they would call me when the Magical crimes guy arrived. I went back to our room to double check everything.

Our door was open when we reached the hallway. I tensed up suspecting the worse, but Cat just nudged me and motioned for us to go on. I heard Chuck's voice and knew it was OK.

"... that sucks little guy! So it's back to Unicorn food for you then, no more pizza?"

"Yeah, she told me I might get a salad now and then. She doesn't even know where we are going! How am I going to watch my shows?"

I pushed the door open and yelled at my Unicorn. "Fergus quit whining to Chuck. Think of it as a road trip." I smiled at Chuck and gave him a big hug. "Hey, don't let short and grumpy here convince you to feed him. He's getting porky with all the pizza."

"I do not look like a pig!" The Unicorn twisted his head back and forth trying to look at his backside.

"Hey, don't look at me. Those pizza parties were all his idea. I just went along for the free food. I'm a guy."

"Of course you are. Are you excited to be going to forensic school?"

"Some. I'd like to do the investigating thing with you and Cat, but it should be pretty cool. I found out I'm supposed to be helping the mobile group this term. Maybe I'll meet that Vampire you told me about."

"Anastasia? I've got her number I could call and ask if you like."

"No, no don't do that. I want fate to be my guide. You said she was hot right?"

"For a Vampire she was. She's also really nice so don't be a guy and hit on her all the time."

"I'll be cool, I promise." He tried to look the part by sucking in his gut and puffing out his chest. It made him look like Popeye.

"Sure you will. Give a hug big guy." He squeezed the life out of me for a moment. "You have my number so feel free to text or call me. I can't do much long distance, but I can try. OK?"

"Sure. Thanks, Aggy."

"It's not forever; we will see each other around. The Bureau isn't that big."

My phone made a noise, and I could feel the vibration. Pulling it out of my pocket I saw that I had a text from the Director. "Hey, my new assignment is here! Director Mills says he's in the main parking lot."

I scooped Fergus up and ignoring his protests put him in my pocket. With Chuck helping we grabbed my bags and headed down to the main lot. I was excited this was the start of my new career.

CAT and I practically ran all the way to the main parking lot. The staff all parked on the left side, but many of them weren't here today. The front spaces were all full as well as the visitor lot. Other than a ratty looking class C camper there weren't any new cars out here. I peered left and right looking for the typical black suburban that many Agents seemed to drive. Or at least they did on the task force last year. I sat down on the steps in front of the school.

"That sucks."

"What they aren't here to get you?"

"It doesn't look like it. I don't see any FBI vehicles anywhere."

"Why would the Director call you if there wasn't someone here for you?"

"I don't know." I pursed my lips and looked over at Cat. She sat down next to me. We watched Chuck come puffing up the sidewalk and set the bags down in front of the RV.

"What in the Hell is in these bags? I don't remember your clothes weighing this much."

"Those are spell components and other materials. I have my clothes right here." I pointed to the bags at my feet.

"Where's your ride?" He looked around the parking lot.

"We were just talking about that. It doesn't seem to be here."

Chuck nodded and started looking at the RV. It was covered in dust and mud and looked filthy. "Um, Agatha?"

I looked in Chuck's direction, and he waved at the RV. Using his hand, he wiped the grime off the driver's side door, and I could see part of the FBI shield on it. The colors were faded and worn.

"I think this is it."

"No way! That is my ride?"

I could hear giggling and looked to my right as Cat rolled up to the steps. "It's not funny Cat! What the hell is that thing?"

"That thing, as you call it, is my home and our investigative unit. You must be Agatha Blackmore. I've heard a lot of good things about you young lady. My name is Special Agent Jack Dalton. Welcome to the team."

We all turned to stare at the older man in a faded suit standing at the top of the stairs. He managed to sneak up on all three of us.

CHAPTER FOUR

We were all staring the man that managed to sneak up on us when the Director appeared.

"Oh, good. You are all here. Jack this is Agatha Blackwood. She is our resident Witch. The short giggling one is Catherine Moore. She is both an Alpha and at the top of our investigative class. The young gentleman over there is Charles Winthrop. He is one of our best new forensic techs. Anastasia herself is going to break him in this year."

I could see the shock on Chuck's face at what Director Mills said. I guess I didn't have to call her after all.

"Yes, I was just introducing myself to them. In answer to your previous question that is our entire world over there. It doesn't look like much but when it was new it was the cutting edge in investigative services. Magical crimes doesn't make the papers as much as the BAU or the crime lab, so our budget is smaller. Most of the money goes for hiring magical support but now we have you. I expect great things from you this year. Maybe you can show an old guy some new tricks."

Cat giggled at what he said, and I narrowed my eyes at him.

"Uh, Jack. You know better than that!" The Director tapped her foot at him. Jack thought for a minute, and his face changed color as we watched.

"I'm so sorry! That was uncalled for. I just mean that once we get in the RV, we can have a good time." Suddenly his face got even redder. "I didn't mean it that way! Damn it; I can't say the right thing, can I? It's just hard."

Even Chuck laughed at that one. "Dude I'd shut up now if I was you."

The Special Agent glanced at the Director and tried not to smile. "I didn't mean it like that, I promise!"

Director Mills just shook her head and turned to walk away. "Come by my office before you leave Jack."

We all watched her leave, and the older man turned back to me. "Let me show you the rig."

He walked down the stairs and opened up the dust-covered door. "Excuse all the dust; I've been on the road a whole lot lately." He stepped up into the rig and told me to come on in.

I peered through the doorway dubiously. Grabbing the railing, I pulled myself into the RV. LED lights lined the walls. There was a computer station and what looked like a basic mini-crime lab set up where the dining area would normally be. There was a small efficiency kitchenette and a couple of couches. Farther back in the truck was a full bathroom with tiny shower. The rear contained a bedroom.

"That's my room back there. You get one of the bunks." He pointed to the side across from the bathroom. Two bunk beds were built into the wall. They were scuffed and had seen hard use.

"We can stop at a local RV place and get you a new mattress. Those do look a bit worn. I usually travel with either one or two hired Mercs. The last two were a bit rough."

I didn't see any bugs, but everything was very dirty. Mud was everywhere. It was even in the bunk I was supposed to sleep in.

"Does everything have to be so dirty?"

Jack gave me a funny look. "Life on the road can be hard. As the intern, clean up is one of your new jobs."

"Really?"

"Yup. I've got cleaning supplies around here somewhere." He began opening some of the cabinets.

"I don't think so." I stepped off the RV back onto the parking lot.

Cat and Chuck having heard the entire conversation with their freaky Cat hearing both looked at me funny. I motioned for them to step back. Grandmother taught me an all purpose cleaning spell that we used every Spring to clean house with. I reached into my pocket for my ever-present salt and herbs.

I raised my hands to the sky and said a prayer to Hestia. She was the Greek Goddess of Hearth and Home. I figured she was appropriate for this circumstance. I scattered the salt mixture and concentrated my will. Speaking the word, "hladhqnd," I brought my hands together and made a sweeping motion. The wind rose, and a breeze rushed through the camper.

"Hey! What the Hell is happening?" Dust and dirt began to billow out of the RV. It resembled what happens when a bag of flour is dropped from a great height. Rain began to fall from the sky, washing the outside of the vehicle. The lettering on the side began to shine. I spoke another word of power, "skýrr," the dents in the sides fixed themselves, and some of the original factory shine came back. Concentrating, I said one more word to finish the job. "Kaun." Steam began to billow from the RV, a line of black scurrying bugs followed it out into the parking lot.

A windblown and coughing Agent stepped from his vehicle and glared at me. "What the hell was that?"

"I cleaned it for you. All done." I pointed at the RV.

It shone. It almost looked brand new in the sunlight. The words Magical Crimes and the FBI seal could be seen clearly. All the dust and grime was now gone.

His jaw fell open as he looked at his official vehicle. "How?"

"Magick of course. Do you have room for all my stuff? I brought all my supplies with me." I pointed to the small pile of bags Chuck brought.

Still staring at the truck and the piles of dirt in the parking lot Agent Dalton nodded. "Sure. Just put them in the bunk you're not using. We will find places later. Can any magical user do this?" He pointed at the RV.

"Sure. It's a fairly common spell. I have a bit more power than most of the hacks you're used to working with. But they could have at least cleaned up after themselves. That is the problem with Mercs. They won't lift a finger unless you pay them."

I told Chuck to put my stuff in the lower bunk. I would take the upper for now. Jack was still staring at the RV when we finished. I gave my friends a big hug. "I'll call you when we get moving. This is going to be fun I think."

"Once he picks his jaw off the ground. You just wowed him, Aggy." Cat gave me another hug. "Come on Chuck, let's get back to the dorm." They waved as they walked away.

"Jack?" I tried to get the Agent's attention. He was down on his knees peering at the underside of the rig.

"Jack? Are you OK?" I tapped him on his arm.

"What? Oh, sorry. How did you do all this? Even the underside hole is fixed! I haven't been able to use that compartment for years."

"It's magick."

"I know that. But how? I've worked with magical support for years, and none of them have ever done anything like this."

"It's magick. We can talk about it later, let's go check in with the Director." I closed the camper door and started walking toward the admin building. I glanced back, and he was just standing there staring at the camper. Laughing, I climbed the stairs. Grandmother would spank me for using so much power on something that trivial, but if I'm going to ride in it, it needs to be clean. Yuck was all I could think of after seeing that bathroom!

My nemesis was at her usual spot behind the information desk.

"Ah, the blond menace is here."

"Hello, witchy poo. We are all out of newts, come to bring us some?"

"I think you are lizard enough for the place don't you think?"

She smiled at me, and we both laughed. We buried the hatchet this past year. She had only been following bad orders after all.

"Hi, Melissa. The guy with his mouth open is Agent Dalton. He's my new trainer."

"We've met. He's a sweetie so don't break him, OK?"

"I'll try not too. We have to see Director Mills before we leave. Is she in?"

"She should be. Want me to check?"

"Nope. We'll surprise her. Thanks."

My new partner finally made it up the stairs and through the doors as I finished with Melissa. We both stared at him as he stepped inside the lobby.

"Ready?" I inclined my head toward the offices.

"Yes, we are going to discuss that back there. I insist."

"Sure. Can we wait until we see the Director?"

He seemed to think for a moment then nodded his head. "Fine, after you."

Leading the way I took us past the various offices and admin workers and approached the Director's door. It was open.

Knocking gently I stuck my head inside. "Director Mills?"

She was at her desk. "Agatha? Please." She gestured to her chairs. Both Dalton and I sat in front of her.

"So, You've met her. What do you think Jack?"

"Well, she fixed the RV and cleaned it up with a spell. I'm not sure what to think." He turned toward me. "You said you would tell me."

"I know you investigate magical crimes but what do you know about Magick?" The way I said it the 'k' was obvious in my pronunciation.

"I don't understand?" He looked at the Director. She shook her head at me.

"This would have been my second lecture if we ever got around to it. Magic is using natural means to trick someone or create an illusion. A few years ago a guy made the Statue of Liberty disappear. That is Magic. What I do is Magick. With a 'kay' at the end. My form of Magick is using ritual or symbols to manipulate the supernatural forces that surround us. I'm sure you, Agent Dalton, and the FBI have run into both kinds."

Dalton nodded his head. "Yes. We have a running list of tricksters and charlatans that run the circuit trying to scam people all the time."

"Right. The Witches Council is aware of them, by the way. They watch for real Wizards that try the same thing. Those they come down hard on and punish accordingly. Real Magick is different. You are used to dealing with the magical dregs of our society. That is what the Russian and Slavic Witches are that you hire. It's not really their fault. As I explained to the Director last year, the Russian magical community was devastated by the Demon War. Their true leaders are either dead or insane. They have no choice but to sell their Magick to the highest bidder." I looked at the Director, and she nodded. Jack was still rocking his head back and forth in thought.

"Agent Dalton?"

He looked up at me. "Sorry. I watched a recording of your lecture, so I remember what you said."

"The big difference is I use natural forces to effect change. That is the simplest definition of Magick. I pray to my Gods, and I invoke the elements using herbs or other spell materials. Using the power of those forces, I concentrate them into power that changes things. Here's an example." I held out my hand and said a silent prayer for control.

My hand began to glow, and a tiny flicker of flame came to life in the center. Very carefully I formed it into a fireball and held out my hand.

I could hear the Director take a sharp breath. "This is a classic fireball. I invoked it by drawing upon the element of fire and a silent prayer to Hephaestus the use of his element." I allowed the ball of flame to exist for a moment more and then reabsorbed the power.

"Now I can call upon the Ull one of the Gods of ice and snow." I held out my hand again, and a ball of ice began to form on it. Soon I held what looked like a snowball.

Setting the ball of ice down on the desk, I stared at my two supervisors. "Understand?"

Agent Dalton reached out a hand and touched the ball of ice. "It's real!"

"Of course it is. That is real Magick. I know you've seen it. Those Mercs do know some of it."

"Sure. I've been working with them for years. Mostly they do spell traces or help us track down rogue Weres. I had one that could make fire, but his didn't look like your's did!"

"For one of them, that's fairly impressive. My Grandmother told me that at one time the Russian Magicians and Wizards were some of the best naturals in the world. If their Volkhvy had not been killed, they might have been much more than they are today. What sort of crime do you investigate?"

Agent Dalton rubbed his chin. I could hear the stubble grating across his hand. I normally couldn't hear all that well and wondered if it was a result of the binding spell I performed with Chuck and Cat just last week. Something to think about later.

"I was going to say magical ones, but that's not true now. I track down rogues and investigate the strange and unusual. I read the file about the Demon cult you exposed last year. That would have been one of mine. I was up in Alaska tracking down a rogue Yeti when the Demon call came in. I allowed the local office to take care of it since they were already set up. I worked the 1990s incursion and was happy you took care of it."

My eyes widened at that. "You fought Demons?"

"Not like you did. There was a British music group that accidentally raised a demon during one of their concerts. It gave each of the performers a certain glamor to sway minds."

"How did you figure out it was demons?" I was running music groups through my head.

"They had a strange following that didn't make a lot of sense.

Each singer had a goofy name. We tracked the Demon to one of the roadies. He was actually working at each concert sucking up energy to raise more. At least that is what the expert I had with me said. After the Demon was slain, the band wasn't the same. They broke up and stopped performing. I think they all got married or something."

"Were the musicians harmed?"

"No. As far as we could tell the Demon just gave them popularity. Without his power anything they tried to sing wasn't quite right after that. The Brits were a bit unhappy with me after that. They had been tracking it too and wanted in on the kill."

"How did you kill it without Magick?"

"It was in a human form. We trapped it in a magical circle and shot it. The Kabbalist I was working with retired after that. He was a rare breed that one."

"If he was a mundane practitioner he was. It takes years to 'get it right' using ceremonial Magick. That is not something anyone should dabble in at all."

They both gave me funny looks. "My Grandmother is the head of our clan and coven. I was fully trained by her before coming here. My magical difficulties put me on the outs by my family, but I was trained in all aspects of Magick. Magick can be very dangerous in the wrong hands."

Agent Dalton looked at the Director. "I'll take her. I will teach her what I know and maybe she can help me on the job."

"I should hope so Jack." She looked at me. "Agatha, Jack and I were like you and Chuck. We were in the same classes together before we went off on our own assignments. He can teach you about investigations, and you can help him with the Magick. The FBI is changing, and for us to change it, we need to make more use of the assets we have. I expect great things from you, Agatha. Make us all proud of you."

"Jack, take care of her and don't let Fergus make you too crazy." She stood up and gave me a big hug which surprised me. "Agatha you have my number. Call if you need something. Technically I have to evaluate you quarterly so don't be a stranger."

Director Mills held the door open for us, and we headed back to the RV. I had to smile when Jack looked at me and asked. "Who's Fergus?"

CHAPTER FIVE

"AGATHA THAT WAS my boss in DC. There was an apparent murder in Richmond that might classify as a Magical crime. It has the locals confused, and they have asked for help. That means us. What I usually do for these is have my magical support scan for spell traces. Now after talking to you, I wonder how many we got wrong over the years. This one is pretty gruesome so prepare yourself for that."

I looked at my new partner and boss and smiled. "I think I can handle it. It can't be worse than the Demon last year."

"True. Is everything reloaded in the back?" He looked over his shoulder at the camper.

"I think so. Using the checklist, I pulled the slides in and disconnected the generator. I went through the whole list. Is there anything not on it?"

"Did you pull the wheel chocks? I don't think those are on the list."

"They aren't. It sounds like I need to make a new list for you." I climbed out of the RV and peered under the back wheels. Plastic yellow wheel chocks were braced under them. I shook my head as I took them out and packed them in one of the compartments. Men.

I did a quick walk-around the RV checking for things that we might have missed before I climbed back inside. I wasn't sure what I was looking for, but I had read the manual for the RV. It was still in its original wrapper in the glove compartment. All I could do was shake my head. Men.

"OK, all set. I think we can get moving now. Do you want me to check the route on the map? My phone has GPS and a cool maps program."

"Maps? We don't need no stinking maps! I've got this." Jack crowed. I just shook my head. This should be fun.

IN THE END, I had to use my phone to find the address. Agent Dalton did have an innate sense of direction, but not once we got inside a city. According to the report we were sent the murder happened inside one of Richmond's best five-star restaurants, Nourriture Chère.

Black and white police cars lined the street, and the entire front of the place was taped off. News vans and onlookers rubbernecking blocked the streets. It was a good thing I cleaned up the RV because now they were focused on us, not the crime scene. Local officers directed us to the best place to park, and Jack maneuvered his rig into place.

"Now, let me do all the talking. This has the potential to become very high-profile. I've already requested assistance from the local office." His tone was all business now.

"I understand. What will they be doing?" I asked.

"We have a lab in here, so I asked for a tech and some investigators. Experience with this has shown they will either send their best or their worst to help me. I'll let you figure out which they send. It's a thing of pride and glory for many of these locals. They want to do the investigation and bask in whatever media attention they get."

"Why? We all work for the same agency, right?"

"It's politics, Agatha. The entire Bureau runs that way, unfortunately. I try to stay out of it as much as possible. My advice to you is to do the same. Let the locals take the credit. They usually will anyway. You cannot control what they do unless DC gets involved. If that happens, they will be the ones taking credit for your work. Stay in the shadows."

"Saying that sounds like you just gave up Jack. Are you sure that's the best way?"

"Sorry, kid. It's just my experience with the whole thing. Don't worry about it for now. I'm the Special-Agent-In-Charge, so I will take whatever heat comes our way. Try to stay out of the way of any political issue that comes up. Now, since we have been requested, we will be in charge here. I try hard not to run roughshod over the locals so be nice. Get your spells ready I have no idea what awaits us inside. The report only said magical death."

I grabbed my bag off the table and slipped my Glock into my shoulder holster. Regulations required me to be armed at all times, but I didn't like wearing my gun while we drove. I'm, sure I would get used to having it eventually. I didn't foresee using it much, but I was an active Agent now. "Fergus be good and watch the RV." I stepped out into my first real assignment as a Probationary Agent.

One of the local police lieutenants was waiting for us as soon as we opened the door.

"Thank god you got here quick!"

Jack stuck out his hand and shook the man's hand. "Hello, Special Agent Jack Dalton. Why? What's happened?"

"The chef here was world famous. His death has attracted international news media, and they are swarming all over the place."

"You are keeping them out of the crime scene?"

"Of course we are! It's just become a real circus. Chef Robbie Lash was a big name around here. He had two different shows on the Eats network."

Jack glanced at me and shook his head. I kept my mouth shut. "Wonderful. Do you have any leads on your end so far?"

"Not really. We have copies of the security camera feeds, and our techs are running them. So far nothing. You have to see the scene to understand. We've never seen anything like it before."

"OK. Make sure we get access to those tapes. I have a few more Agents on the way so watch for them."

We pushed our way through the crowd of newsies and ducked under the yellow caution tape. The restaurant was done in a French Provincial style and was very fancy inside. The front doors had heavy cast iron handles and hinges. A large oil painting of the Chef was in the front entrance. I had recognized the name; Grandmother watched his shows.

"The scene is in the kitchen. We tried to leave it as is."

"Did the coroner already remove the body?" The young officer froze at that. He stopped again and just stared at us.

"Didn't you get a description? The body is melted to one of the tables. We have no idea how even to remove it much less see how it was done." He pointed to the swinging door I assumed led to the kitchen.

The smell is what struck me the moment I stepped into the kitchen. Grandmother's kitchen always smells of spices and citrus. This one smelled of death and pain. Several officers were standing around staring and a police photographer was puking in a bucket. Not a good sign.

Spotting the sergeant in charge Jack tapped him on the arm. "Excuse me, Sergeant?"

"Feds?"

"Yes..."

The Sergeant barely spoke to us. He yelled at the officers to clear out. "The scene is all yours." He turned and left in a hurry.

I finally spoke. "That was rude of him."

Jack nodded his head in agreement. "Typically they don't like us, but I agree with you."

We both stepped around into the main part of the kitchen line and saw what had the locals so shaken up. Robbie Lash was literally melted into the metal table. The cutting board and table top were part of him somehow. It was like a gruesome statue. The upper half of the Chef's body was metallic and the lower half flesh. At first, I thought it might have been a spell gone wrong but as far as I knew Lash was mundane.

"Have you ever seen anything like this before Agatha?" Jack looked over at me. I had bent down and was looking at the underside of the table. I could see the other half of the Chef's face impressed into the metal.

"No. Not at all. I was thinking it could have been a spell gone horribly wrong, but he wasn't a Wizard. Or at least I didn't think he was. I need to do a diagnostic spell. Hold on a moment."

Surprisingly I wasn't grossed out by the dead guy stuck in the table. I think my experiences with the Demon Cult last year broke me of that. It was nasty but bearable. I said a prayer to my Goddess and focused my will on the diagnostic spell I had learned. Using what a gamer would call my mage-sight I glimpsed a brief magical world in the kitchen.

"Jack he may not have been a magician, but someone or something sure was in here." I opened my eyes and stared at the Agent.

"What do you mean?"

"Just about everything in here has the glow of Magick to it. I need to walk around."

I began following the magical traces on all the appliances. Even the oven had a glow to it. Grandmother had warned me about zapping mundane building items. Usually bad or unexpected results occurred when we tried to enhance those items. Too many Magick users had been swayed by the movie industry to attempt a flying car or magical bed-knob.

The Magick seemed to be concentrated on the coolers. The door to both the freezer and the walk-in glowed brightly in my sight.

"Over here Jack. The coolers glow like they are on fire." I pointed at both the large metal doors.

Remembering the report from last year he voiced my worries. "Do you think it's Demonic?"

"The colors aren't the same for Demon activity. That door just felt evil. I don't get the same vibes from these." I slipped on some rubber gloves just to be sure and reached for the door.

Out of the corner of my eye, I saw Jack reach for his weapon as the door opened. Nothing leapt out at us. No creepy clowns or demonic visages decorated the inside of the door. I stuck my head through the vinyl strips and looked in. I saw a light switch and flipped it on. The shelves in the cooler glowed with Magickal light. Uh oh.

"Jack I think I know what killed the Chef."

"Did you find something?" Stepping into the cooler with me, Jack looked around at the bins of fruits and vegetables.

Reaching into a bin, I held up a piece of fruit. "This is a Fae apple. I think our Chef pissed off the local Fae and they killed him for it."

"Fae? You mean like fairies?" He looked at me like I was crazy.

"Yes. They do exist. Just about all the fruit and vegetables in here are from their gardens. Either Lash had a contact, or he stole all these. Stealing from the Fae is a death sentence. They take offense easily."

"Wait, you're saying the Fae are real?"

"Of course they are real. The court's had an ambassador to the President after the first World War. Don't you read history? I've looked at mundane history books; they do mention the Fae. You have been doing this job for over a decade. You haven't run into the Fae in all that time?"

"No, I haven't. None of my support magicians ever mentioned them to me."

"Hmm. Interesting. Grandmother deals with them all the time. They come to her for rare herbs and some Magickal solutions. I can read their language better than I speak it, but I can get by."

"So what about the vegetables? Why is having them a bad thing?"

"It's what they eat to preserve their long life and vitality. Imagine you had something that would cure cancer, and you couldn't share it without killing off your entire family. Would you give it away or even tell anyone about it?"

"This stuff cures cancer?"

"No. It keeps Magickal beings alive. Remember when I talked about elemental powers?" The Agent nodded at me. "The Fae are related to those powers. Several of our people believe that they are some of the older Gods and Goddesses whose names we have forgotten. They live and breathe Magick. The food that they eat is Magick in all of its properties. The items in this cooler and I assume the other are priceless. In mundane terms, there is over a hundred million sitting right here. There are Wizards that would level this town to gain what is here. We are sitting on a pile of dynamite."

"Seriously? It's boxes of vegetables!"

"Look what happened to the Chef if you don't believe me. If the Fae killed him, I don't understand why they left the fruit... "I stared at the cooler door. "Do you have a magnet on you? Never mind." I closed my eyes and recited a cantrip I knew. The door to the cooler glowed gold for just a moment.

"Damn. OK, this door is made of cold iron. It's not steel or aluminum like most coolers. This front part of the door and the handle are made from pure iron."

"Why is that important and how did you know?"

"Did you see the door change color for just a moment?"

"Yes."

"Iron burns gold when exposed to an electric arc. That is how I knew it was made of iron. Iron and steel are deadly to the Fae. Many old world superstitions speak of nailing a horseshoe above the door or carrying a rusty nail with you. It gives you protection from the Fae. Ferrous material is what they fear, cold iron the most. Only humans can forge it in its pure form. Just grabbing this door would have killed a Fae warrior. Stepping inside an iron box? No way they would have done that. It makes me wonder how many they lost just getting in here."

"Why do you say that?"

"Remember the front doors? They had cast iron handles. All the candelabras looked to be iron too. Even this kitchen. Look at all the stainless steel. It's everywhere. He knew exactly what he was doing. He thought he was safe. Want to bet he was living here somewhere?"

My new boss was nodding his head. "You're pretty sharp for a newb. I think this is going to work. OK, you lead on this one."

"Me?" I stared at Jack with very wide eyes.

"Just kidding. I've got the lead. But, you will stick with me on this. I know nothing about the Fae. Nothing at all. Hell, I didn't even believe they were real. When the other Agents get here, we will delegate. What is your recommendation for the vegetables?"

I just stared at him for a moment. "Gosh. Let me think a moment. I can call my grandmother and have her put me in contact with the Fae she knows, but they are not the same as the ones here. There are many tribes. Technically they have one ruler for each Realm, but they don't normally involve themselves in daily life or anything really."

"Realm?"

"Sorry. The Fae are split between kingdoms. Think Summer and Winter. Good and Evil doesn't work for the Fae. They are all both Good and Evil. Their rulers are crazy powerful and are like nuclear bombs in the ratio of power. We do not want to involve them. Ever."

"OK. Call your grandmother, and I will call my boss. We will meet in the middle OK?" I nodded and whipped out my cell phone. I wandered over to the other side of the kitchen out of the way and dialed Grams. She must haves sensed something because she picked up after the first ring.

"Hello, Agatha."

"Hello, Grams. That's creepy how you do that you know."

"What has happened?"

"OK. Straight to the point then. I'm at a crime scene, and a mundane is dead. He was melted to a steel table."

"Is he one of ours? Did he cast something that went haywire?"

"No. It was some form of Elfshot."

"Oh. Do you know why?"

I took a deep breath. "He has a cooler full of Fae fruits and vegetables."

"For real? Child what are you involved in! Who was the Chef?"

"I can't reveal details of an investigation, but he was your favorite. Is there any way you can put me in contact with them? The place they are stored is cold iron. If word gets out of what is here?"

"I understand dear. They are difficult to deal with. I know you remember the ones that come here."

"Yes, Ma'am. I need to try. The battle over what is here could destroy an entire city. It can't be allowed to get loose."

"Stay safe child. Expect a call." I stood and stared at the phone for a moment. I could hear Jack, and he didn't sound very happy.

"I understand. Yes, Sir. Yes. Yes. She is working out just fine. In the six short hours we have been together I have learned about things that I have never encountered after fifteen years in the field. Yes. Yes. No, Sir! I understand. Yes. Thank you, Sir." He closed his flip phone and stared at me shaking his head.

"Well, that was interesting. The Fae still have an Embassy in Washington. Officially. No one has been seen entering or exiting it in over seventy years of observation. My bosses are aware of Fae communities in the United States. That was complete news to me, by-the-way. I am to follow your lead in this. They said to protect the... items from harm. I assume you can do that?"

"That? Easily. Grandmother has promised to pass my request along to her contact. She said they would call me. That will not get us our killers or lead us to those that supplied the Chef the items, to begin with. We need to figure out if he served any of it. This could get messy."

"Do me a favor and protect the items first. We can work on the other stuff next."

I thought for a moment and patted my working bag. "I have enough supplies to do something. Give me about twenty minutes?"

"That's fine. Hurry. I hate to think we caused Richmond to burn a second time."

"Yes, Sir." I dug into my bag and started preparing the shield spell. I didn't have Grandmother's traps to lay down like at my lab, but I could do something. I dragged an empty cart over to the doors and placed it between them. Carefully selecting candles, I began sketching out my circle around the coolers. They were built -ins so I could ward the outside wall as well and be safe.

I assumed Jack stepped outside to search for our missing agents. But then I heard voices.

"Whoa! Narly. Check out this guy!" I glanced over my shoulder and saw three young looking men in suits and an older woman. Thinking back to the conversation I had with Jack I wondered where they would fall. I ignored them and went back to work. I finished my sketching and began to arrange the candles. I muttered the basic spell as I laid each candle and scattered my herbs and salt.

"Hey, are you Agent Blackmore?" I glanced at the new Agents, but I needed to finish.

"I'm talking to you! Stand up when a higher ranking agent enters the room! Hey! I'm talking to you." I heard footsteps as the arrogant woman approached me. I paused for a split second and muttered "létta" and pointed a finger. The Agent was frozen to the floor. I went back to my casting.

"What the hell! Hey, you! That's illegal. I can arrest you for that!"

Jack stepped into the room in the next moment shutting her up. "What in the name of all the Gods is the racket in here? This is an investigation, not a schoolyard. What is going on?"

They all began talking at once. "One at a damn time. Shut Up! Now." He pointed at the youngest looking one. "You, tell me what happened."

"Well, we walked into the scene and saw that girl over there. Agent Sims asked her if she was Agent Blackmore and she didn't answer. Agent Sims then yelled at her and still no answer. She tried marching over there to grab her and stopped frozen to the floor. Then you came in. Sir."

Jack looked at the woman I froze. "Agent Sims. What did I tell you to do?"

"You said to go into the kitchen and while not touching anything make sure that Agent Blackmore was not bothered."

"So why were you bothering her?" I stopped listening to the conversation after that. I needed to concentrate.

I began my incantation repeating the words as forcefully as I could. My voice escalated after each stanza. I felt as though I was screaming the last words. I could feel the power building it was being magnified by the contents of the coolers. I cast the final phrase and held my breath. Like one of those block games my cousins played, I felt the segments of my spell lock into place with a click. I let out my breath.

Jack and the other Agents were all staring at me with very wide eyes. "OK, It's done. The shield is up."

"Jack, did you hear me?" Jack shook his head for a moment.

"Sorry Agent Blackmore. Can you?" He pointed at Agent Sims.

I made a hand motion and said "ganga." The Agent was now free. "Sorry about that. I needed to finish, and I couldn't stop without starting over again."

"Is it locked?"

"Yes. A tank couldn't drive through it now. Remember, except under very rare circumstances, what one Witch does, another cannot undo. Ever."

"Ever?"

"There are workarounds for everything. It's like cutting a tree down. Some use an Axe; some use a bulldozer. Different approaches. This will hold until someone comes to get it." I decided not to trust the new Agents.

Jack turned to the local Agents. "As you may have already guessed Agent Blackmore is the FBI's first official Witch sanctioned by the Witches Council. She has a bit more to offer than our usual hired help. The dead man in the table is the renowned Chef and restaurant owner Robbie Lash. We don't know who or what caused this at present. Agent Jackson is it?" The Surfer sounding Agent raised his hand.

Jack shook his head. "Jackson it's your job to figure out how to get him to the morgue. The Coroner has been here and released the body. Figure something out. Try not to let any of the press see that. Agent Sims, take Agent Reynold here and figure out where the Chef sleeps at night. He may have a residence in the building. Find it. We will need to get a warrant for anyplace we find. Even though Magical crimes takes precedence, this guy was a celebrity. Get moving."

He waited until the others had left before stepping closer to me. "It's locked?"

"Yes. For now, it's safe. He might have something in his home, but I doubt it. He knew what he had and was trying to hide it."

"That is my feeling too. What did you do to Sims?"

"Just a freeze spell. Sorry, she was about to mess everything up."

"It's fine. Try not to do that to fellow Agents. Now lesson time. Did you understand what I said about precedence?"

"I heard you mention it. Why?"

"Little known fact about this division of the FBI. We were established in the 1970s. Magical crimes became a bit more noticeable with TV taking over from the radio as a way of seeing the news. Congress passed a law that gives us precedence in any investigation that contains a magical crime. It has to be real magic, not an illusion. What that means is this has become our case, not the locals."

Looking around, I stared at the body of the chef. "What do you want me to do now?"

"Are you OK to still work after doing all that?" He wiggled his fingers.

I smiled at him. "Yes, I can still work. I would need to rest a moment before fighting demons, but I can handle anything else."

"Good. I want you to go back to the RV and start writing up what it was you did. Everything runs on a sea of paper in the government.

One nice thing about us is our reports are classified top secret. Keep your phone handy and let me know if you get a call from the Fae."

I thanked him and made my way past the Agent working to move the table. I didn't envy him that job at all. Keeping my eyes firmly on the RV I walked past the crowds of Newsies and onlookers. It seemed that there were even more than before here. Using my key, I stepped inside to the RV and collapsed into a chair. I sat there for a moment just breathing. I looked around. Something smelled like popcorn!

Music was coming from Fergus's barn, so I looked inside. He was sitting on a bag of popcorn watching his phone play ZBZ the raunchy celebrity stalker channel.

"Fergus! How did you get popcorn?"

"I made it in the microwave over there." I looked at the kitchenette. The microwave was located above the stove about five feet from the floor.

"Really? Seriously. How did you get popcorn?"

"I made it over there in the kitchen. Want some?"

"After you've been sitting on it? No. It looks like we are going to be here for a while. The Fae are involved with this one."

"The Fae? Agatha stay away from those people! You remember the looks I got the last time they visited at the house?"

I did. They were fascinated by a micro Unicorn and wanted to buy him from me.

"Don't worry; you are an official FBI Unicorn now. You are not for sale."

"I'm official? Do I get a badge?"

"No, you do not get a badge. Go back to your trash TV." Unicorns. I felt a vibration and pulled out my phone. The number was unknown. I sighed and answered it.

"Hello?"

CHAPTER SIX

"Miss Blackmore?"

"Yes, this is Agent Blackmore."

"Hello. You may call me Cullasben. Your Grandmother asked me to contact you on a subject of great urgency. What is it that you wish?"

I tried to remember anything and everything I ever learned about the Fae. "I am on assignment in Richmond, Virginia with the FBI. A mundane was murdered magically yesterday. The man had in his possession a large amount of fruits and vegetables that are of a Fae nature." There was nothing but silence on the phone.

"I have warded the refrigeration units to shield them from harm and further theft. However, that leaves them in my possession. I require assistance or disposal of the items. Unfortunately, I don't have contact information for any of the Hosts present here." One of the problems with dealing with Magical creatures and beings is asking for help. You cannot be too direct, and you should never, ever thank them.

"Well-a-day. That is most interesting Miss Blackmore. The Host you should be dealing with in that part of this fine world is of a frosty nature. I do not, myself, have direct dealings with his kind. However, I can be of assistance to contact someone who can help you. Do you wish my help?"

There it was. Asking for help from the Fae is a loaded question. Their help isn't always helpful and can be malicious.

"Do you promise to neither hurt nor harm me or those associated with me? I am attempting to correct a wrong not start a conflict."

"Of course. My clan will neither hunt, hinder, or harm the person of Agatha Blackmore and those she holds dear. Is that clear enough Milady?"

"I believe so. Who shall my contact be for those of frost kind?"

"He should be there now. Look for a Jack-in-Green. He is to be your escort. Fare thee well Miss Blackmore." I heard the phone click.

I was cursing up a storm when Jack stepped into the RV with Agents Sims and Reynolds. Stopping my exposition on life, in general, I looked up at Jack.

"Problems?"

"Both yes and no. Can we tell them?" I pointed at the two Agents.

"Go ahead. We need to be sure none of the press gets this information." He looked around through the RV's tinted windows.

"That's easy, actually." I pointed at the windows and mumbled the cantrip I used in school to deaden the room of listening devices. "All fixed."

"That fast?"

"Yup." I pretended to blow smoke off my finger.

Jack turned to the two locals and began to describe what we figured happened. He did not tell them what was in the coolers. He looked at me. "Anything else Agent Blackmore?"

"Yes. Do you have any questions before we continue?" I looked at the two Agents who were staring at us like we were crazy people.

Agent Sims held up her hand. "I have a question. Did you just say that Fairies killed the Chef?"

"Yes, he did. The spell that caused him to meld with the table was a form of Elf-Shot."

"That's crazy! Fairies don't exist."

"So Witches and Weres don't exist? I know the Richmond bridge has at least one Troll colony living under it. How can you not believe in Fairies?"

"I've never seen one before. Nobody has! I mean I learned about them in school, but they don't exist anymore!"

"Just because you haven't seen something doesn't mean it isn't really there. That is one of the problems with Magical crimes. Belief."

"Mooo. What the hell is all the racket out here? Can't you see I'm trying to sleep?" Fergus took that moment to step out of his barn. The micro - Unicorn stared at the Agents and looked up at me. "Who are these two? Find some new cannon fodder?"

"Fergus say hello to Agents Sims and Reynolds."

My Unicorn snorted and returned to his barn. The door went "Mooo." We could hear Rap music start up from inside the toy barn.

"That was Fergus, my familiar." Both Agents eyes moved away from the barn back to me.

"Now. Fairies. My contact called me back, and the local Host are followers of Winter."

"Is that bad?" Jack kept one eye on the Agents and one on me.

"Maybe. My Grandmother usually only deals with Summer. The Winter Fae can be more trouble. Their Host contains the darker elements of the Fae world. Goblins and Trolls make up their army. I have been promised an escort to meet with them."

"Is that dangerous?"

"The one that is providing the escort will not allow me or mine to be harmed during the journey. He could not speak for the Winter Fae. I would have to negotiate with them too."

"Can you protect us? What I mean is can your Magic protect us from them?"

"Maybe. I have not ever had to in the past. My encounters with the Fae was an associate of my Grandmothers. I believe that none will wish to cross her, but they still may try something."

Jack looked puzzled by what I said. "Why would they risk pissing off the Witches Council and your Grandmother?"

"Do you know the story of the scorpion and the fox?"

"OK. I understand you now." Jack nodded his head.

Agent Sims looked back and forth between the two of us. "What story? I don't understand? Reynolds do you know what they are talking about?" Agent Reynolds had been peeking through the barn windows at Fergus, and he jumped at hearing his name.

I smiled. "It's a modern fable. A scorpion wanted to cross the river. A fox came along and told him he would carry him on his back if the scorpion promised not to sting him. The scorpion agreed and climbed on the fox. Halfway across the river, the scorpion stung the fox. Starting to drown the fox asked the scorpion why? He said 'It's my nature.' The parable is that something that is naturally vicious will not change."

Nodding her head, Agent Sims looked up at me. "I see. So these Fairies are bad guys, and they will attack us anyway just because?"

"Pretty much. Think of it as going into a maximum security prison unarmed. They will attack you just because."

Catching my attention, Jack waved at me. "Where is our contact supposed to meet us?"

I looked out the front window of the RV. "See the guy dressed like a tree throwing pine cones at the press?"

Outside the RV and behind the caution tape were over a hundred news cameras and photographers. You would almost think they were shooting a political ad as much commotion this Chef's death was causing. Along with the newsies were several hundred tourists and rubberneckers. Working the crowd were Bogies dressed as modern-day troubadours complete with musical instruments and painted faces. A taller man was dressed as a tree representing the Jack-in-the-green. He was picking cones off his body and dancing as he threw them at unsuspecting news reporters.

The other Agents all looked. "It's that guy. I was told to look for the Jack-in-the-green, and he's the only one that fits."

"Why him?"

"Because the Fae have a sense of humor? A twisted one." As we watched the tree man was confronted by several of the local police officers who were trying to get him to stop.

"Do you mind if I try and rescue him?"

"Go try."

I stepped out of the RV and ran over to the Richmond police officers.

"I don't understand. Why do I have to leave? I already have leaves! See?" The tree man did a little dance that involved swinging his branches. The Bogies all clustered around played their music to accompany him. I felt a touch of Magick in the air. Before my eyes, the air shimmered and rippled. The music was magic.

"Excuse me?" I tapped one of the officers on the arm. They were trying to encircle the painted men and were yelling at them to stop playing.

"Excuse me?" I tapped the man again. This time he looked in my direction and told me to back off.

I concentrated my will this time. Glaring at the officer who ignored me I snapped my fingers and said a word of power for them to stop. For a second, time seemed to stop in front of the restaurant. All of the officers and Bogies froze for just a moment.

"Oops, I used too much." I reached through the boys in blue and grabbed the tree man.

"Hey let go of me." The Jack-in-the-Green looked in my direction. "Ah, the Witch. Took you long enough."

"Come along; I have to let them go before someone sees too much." He pushed past the officers and followed me at a jog to the RV.

As we walked away, I unfroze the officers. Pushing the Tree in front of me, I confronted the now confused officers. "Gentleman. My name is Agent Blackmore. We need to speak to the Tree for a moment. You can have him back when we are done if you like?"

The lead officer looked around, and the rest of the Bogies had disappeared. "Just tell him to leave the Newsies alone."

Pointing at the door, I told the tree to go inside.

"Well a day Agents. My name is Jack!" He was bowing with a leafy flourish as I stepped in and closed the door behind me.

"Well met and merry meet Jack. Are you our escort to the lands of frost and snow?" All three of the Agents stared at me.

"The dark lands are cold and wrought with danger. Is it wise to take such as these there?" He looked pointedly at the two local agents.

"My choice of companions is not my own. I am but an escort such as you."

The tree inclined his head to me, and I returned the gesture. Are you prepared to journey?"

"Is there to be contest or tourney?"

"Nay. I was told your request was one of urgency. We must haste for the hour is growing old." He looked at us expectantly.

"Sir, we need to decide who goes and who stays. We only have one window of opportunity if you wish answers and disposition for the case." I tapped my wrist to signify time. I hoped he would understand me.

"Agent Reynolds, did you locate the Chef's residence?"

"Yes, Sir. It is on the second floor of the restaurant."

"Good. Did you request a warrant and search it yet?"

Agent Sims answered for Reynolds who looked a bit confused. "I called it in to Judge Winston, but they are dragging their feet for some reason."

"Thank you, Agent Sims. I will take care of it. Since you know the local lay of the land I am going to leave you in charge of Reynolds and Jackson when he gets finished moving the body. I want the entire kitchen processed along with the Chef's apartment. Leave both the cooler and the freezer alone. They contain illegal substances that the

Chef stole from the people that killed him. Agent Blackmore has secured them for now."

Agent Sims had a gleam in her eye. "Is it drugs? Is that what went down in there? A drug deal?"

"It wasn't drugs. But it may have been a business deal gone bad. Hold down the fort, do your assignment and do not talk to the press. Understand? No news conferences and no press."

"Understood. Come along Reynolds." Both Agents nodded to me and left the RV. I glanced at my boss.

"Do you think they will disobey you?"

"Probably. If not them, their local boss. That mention of drugs won't stay on the down-low. Eh. It will make a good cover story." At my look, he smiled "Like we can tell the public that the Chef was killed because he cooked the wrong vegetable?"

"True. OK, where do we need to go?" I looked at the Tree man for direction.

"Simplicity in itself. The alley behind whence to foul deed was done holds the answer."

"Anyway, you can shed the greenery?" The Jack-in-the-green only smiled at me. "I guess not. Let's try handcuffs?" I looked toward my boss Jack, not the tree Jack.

"Sounds good." I tried not to enjoy zip tying our escort, but I did a little. "Let's go."

We led the man past the local police and the news reporters in a reverse perp-walk. The volume outside increased to that of a roar as hundreds of voices screamed out questions about our 'captive.' I was sure that what we were doing was being beamed around the world to every news agency.

The locals didn't try to stop us as we re-entered the restaurant and passed through to the back door. "OK. Where is the entrance?"

The alleyway was crowded with dumpsters and grease collection vats. For such a fancy place I was surprised by the filth in the alley. Our shoes made sticky sounds as our prisoner led us to the juncture between the buildings. He held up his hands.

"Sorry." I cut him loose.

"Do you like movies? This one is my favorite." He produced a branch from his costume and tapped out a pattern on the bricks of the building. They began to spin in upon themselves, and a doorway opened up to us.

"Hey, isn't that from that kid's movie Harry something or other?"

"It is. The Fae cannot create original works they only copy. Do not be surprised once we pass through. You may recognize some things." I glanced at our guide. "Is this actually Underhill or something else?"

"Close. A pale comparison as you might call it. The local Host have a fondness for what you will see. You will be quite safe. Passage is given." He stepped into the gloom and disappeared.

"Here we go. Hold on to your wits." I grabbed Jack and pulled him through the doorway with me.

CHAPTER SEVEN

THE TRANSITION WAS INSTANTANEOUS, like stepping into a strange room. We found ourselves in a dark primeval forest surrounded by what I can only call horror-movie trees. They were the classic creepy leafless trees that creaked and moaned in the wind. Every shadow evoked those hidden secret fears of dark fantasy everyone experienced at least once in their life. Faint shrieks could be heard in the distance muffled by the whistling of the wind through the trees. The whole place gave me the shivers.

"What is this place?" I glanced at Agent Dalton.

"This is the gateway to the dark realm. Welcome to Faerie." The Jack-in-the-green had lost his tree-like visage. He now wore huntsman style clothing.

"Agatha, have you been here before?"

"No. Grandmother has described it. All of this is supposed to scare us."

Our escort reached out and broke off a branch. The tree rustled and moaned in response. "This is one of the more out-of-touch realms. Be alert here Miss Blackmore."

I looked closer at our guide. "Do I know you?"

"Maybe, maybe not. Come along we must not tarry here. These woods hold far worse than trees. Best not to wake the beasts." He stepped onto the trail that appeared suddenly and began to walk. Agent Dalton and I warily followed after him. The trail was anything but straight and narrow. It wound its way through the woods over hill and dale twisting at times through tight brush. Our guide steadfastly stayed on the path and never allowed us to linger at any specific spot. Finally, the trees gave way to a snow-covered tundra that seemed to stretch out for miles.

Wind whistled across the tundra causing my hair to fly in front of my eyes. Brushing it away, I pulled it into a ponytail and secured it. Goosebumps ran up my arms as I caught a chill from something other than the wind. The 'caw' of a crow made me look up suddenly. The night sky was alive with fireflies and strange formations of stars.

"It is here that I leave you." The former Jack-in-the-green was now stood as an ancient man wearing a robe leaning upon a walking stick. Only one of his eyes could be seen peering out from under a large wide-brimmed hat.

"Why?"

The old man's eye was white in color and what could be seen of his face was wrinkled and scarred. His eye looked in my direction; I could see a brief smile cross his face. "I cannot enter the cold realm without invitation. Just ahead are two crows. They hold the doors. Bargain with them. I shall wait here until you return." He pointed a shaky finger in the direction of the blowing wind.

Jack stood in front of the old man staring at him in awe. "Come on Jack."

I reached out and grabbed Jack pulling him toward me. "We have to go."

"Is he...?"

"I don't know. Grandmother never told me to expect anything like this. Come on. This is our only chance for answers."

We left the old man standing in the snow and trudged forward.

Just over the rise stood what appeared to be a Norse longhouse. A pair of giant crows stood guard on either side of the door.

Jack took the lead as we trudged through ever deepening snow. The wind had picked up, and cold seeped through the thin material of my suit jacket. I cast a warming spell that helped offset the ever increasing chill.

"Are those crows or are they people?" I peered through the blowing snow. From here they looked like giant crows, but as we got closer, I could see it was a costume.

The two costumed warriors straightened as we stepped closer. The wind died down as well as the snow. Jack started to step forward and the 'crows' reached for weapons. I put my hand on his arm to prevent him from drawing his gun. "Let me speak to them first."

"Greetings. We come to ask a boon. May we have free passage?" My speech was English, and the door wardens ignored me. I tried again in Elvish. Once again I was ignored. Carefully I asked again in Old Norse. The taller of the two perked up and cocked his head to listen. I once again asked for a boon.

The guards opened the doors and stood back.

"Is that it?" Jack was staring at the crows.

"It may be. They didn't reply though so be wary." I followed Jack as he stepped into the long-house.

Torches burned along the walls at the entrance. It took a moment for my eyes to focus in the flickering light. Benches lined the walls. Over a dozen Fae warriors sat staring at us. In the center of the hall was a raging bonfire. Smaller cook fires took up space on either side of the main fire. Craftsmen worked along the edges of the fires. Beyond these activities were a pair of occupied thrones. All activity stopped as we stepped into the room. The doors boomed closed behind us.

"Who comes?" The language was English.

"Agents Blackmore and Dalton of the American FBI." The warriors along the walls all sat forward. We could see that that most did not appear to be human.

"Come forward Agents of the FBI." Carefully we stepped

around the craftsmen and approached the throne. The King was a large dark skinned Fae warrior. He wore what appeared to be the skin of a polar bear over his shoulders. His armor sparkled and gleamed in the flickering light. To his left was an elf stripped to the waist and nailed to a beam. He hung four or five feet off the ground. I grimaced at the sight of the blood eagle.

Jack and I tried not to look at the torture victim as we approached the throne. Stopping at a respectable distance, we stood and stared up at the king.

"Why have you come?"

"A man was murdered in the human city of Richmond. The magic used to kill him was of the Fae. We would like to know his crimes and seek the one that performed it."

"His death is known to us. The death was required as punishment for theft and betrayal."

"I understand the theft. We discovered the fruits of the Fae. How did he betray?"

"This man came to us with a challenge. A challenge of wits against Hádhon our Royal cook. The prize was a knife of extraordinary appeal. The challenge was fought, and he gained what he wished."

Jack and I exchanged looks. "So Chef Lash came here to your hall and challenged Hádhon to a cooking challenge? Is that what you mean?"

"Was I not clear? He betrayed our trust and stole from our Royal stores. I ordered the return of what he stole and an appropriate punishment be exacted."

"Great King. The punishment was just. How did he gain access to your stores? Are they not guarded by your strongest warriors?" When in doubt kill them with kindness and praise.

"Treachery most foul was perpetrated by Hádhon! He conspired with the human to steal the food from our very mouths. He has paid and will continue to pay for his desires." The King pushed at the hanging man with his scepter. With his lungs glistening in the firelight groans could be heard coming from the victim. "He hangs here as tribute to the Gods for his deceit."

Jack was staring in horror. The cook's lungs had been pulled out of his body and were sucking air. He continued to groan as he rocked back and forth.

"So Hádhon and the human chef stole the stores for profit? Why would Hádhon do that?"

"He wished to travel with humans. The human showed him images of world competition and foods beyond ken."

I nodded. The food programs on Eats Network did look like fun to compete in.

"This human convinced Hádhon to provide him with forbidden fruits to gain entrance to this world of TV."

"Your Majesty that is why we are here. The forbidden items are in our possession. We would like to ensure their safe return to you and yours. How do we do that?" I glanced at Jack and nodded. He was getting the hang of talking to these Fae.

The Fae looked down at us with eyes that gleamed. "You have the items. You. Give them to us. Give them to us now!"

Crap. "Your Majesty. They are at the human cook's restaurant under a protective shield. Lash had them stored in a vault made of cold iron. He planned his theft well. We believe he intended to feed them to humans. Do you have a trusted agent we can give them to?" The King leaned further forward on his throne his beady eyes burned as they peered at me.

"My people are forbidden to deal with those on the surface. How did you find my kingdom? What spy gave you my location?"

All around the room the warriors leaned forward at the mention of a spy. Rustling could be heard in the dark corners of the hall. I swallowed nervously. This could turn bad very quickly.

"Majesty, we were led to the edge of your lands by a Jack-in-the-Green provided to us by Cullasben. He awaits us even now." The King made a motion with his hand, and we felt a rush of air as the doors opened and then slammed shut again.

"I shall speak to this Green man of yours. You may sit." He pointed to chairs that appeared in front of the fire. We carefully sat facing the king. Agent Dalton leaned in to speak to me, and I grabbed his arm. Shaking my head, I placed a finger on my lips. The King did not give us leave to speak. Seeing this, the King and his warriors began to laugh.

How fast can a Fae warrior run through snow? That was one of the many questions I asked myself as we sat there. The fire was in back of us, the King in front. No escape without a fight. I could feel the Fae King's Wards surrounding us. I might possibly be able to freeze the warriors and maybe fight my way out the doors with my Magick. But I couldn't leave Jack to the mercy of the King. I said a silent prayer to my Goddess for help, for luck I prayed to Odin as well.

The doors opened with a swirl of dust and blowing snow. Light streamed into the hall amid cries of "close the door." The heat from the fires melted the frost from the Fae warrior as he passed through the hall dripping chunks of ice. Behind him came a cloak covered figure leaning upon a walking stick. The doors slammed shut behind them. Smoke and steam from the fires filled the room. It was a death sentence to turn your back on the King without leave. I craned my head trying to see who the warrior returned with. Was it the Green man, the hunter, or the old man? Which would it be?

"What is this you bring me?" The King stood and towered over his warrior. "This is no Green Man! Who are you that enters into my hall?"

The cloaked figure swept off his covering with a swirl. A grizzled figure stood in the hall. Like the Green Man he wore branches and green. Like the huntsman he was clad in leather and fur. Like the old man he had one eye and a wide brim hat. His one eye gleamed for a moment in the light of the fire; he gave off a strange aura of power. Stepping forward as if to warm his hands he looked up at the King from under his hat. "I am but a wandering traveler, lord. My task was to bring you these two lost souls in need of assistance. It was you that asked me inside."

"Wandering traveler indeed. I know who you are. Your games are not needed here one-eye. This is my domain, not your's! I wish for you to leave us and go!"

"Not without my charges. They come with me."

"No! The humans stay! They have stolen from me, and I want my storehouse returned!"

"How can they do as you ask without leaving? Give them to me."

"No!" The King reached for his sword. Many of the warriors in the hall were already armed.

The one-eyed man's eye crackled with power. "They are already under my protection. They return with me. I will ensure that your fruit is returned."

The sound of crows could be heard in the rafters of the hall. I looked up to see the shining eyes of dozens of dark as night birds. The King looked as well, he backed up and sat down on his throne. He gave his former cook a shove. The near death being choked and moaned as he gasped for breath. "A bargain we shall have then. Return what was taken, and we will forget your trespass, this time."

"A bargain it is then. I and my charges will take leave of you King Dolon of the Dusk Fae." The King nodded his head and made a hand motion. The doors were opened, and the warriors returned to their benches. "Come mortals; we must leave. Now."

I touched Jack, and we both stood. Being careful not to offend the King we walked backward then turned. I pointed toward the door and then touched my lips again.

Our protector and guide followed us out. "I believe I mentioned bargaining with the guards before entering? Always remember to bargain before doing something in the Fae lands. Many hidden dangers."

"But..." He held up his hand.

"Wait until we are free of this place. Too many mistakes can be made by the unwary." He motioned for us to lead. I could see the edge of the forest in the distance; it looked farther away than getting here was.

We could see the remnant of our previous path, so that is what we followed. The tree line stood just as dark and gloomy as before. I stopped and stomped the snow off my legs and feet.

"It is time for you to return." The old man pointed to the dark path. "Put your feet on the path and return to your own Realm."

"What of the Fae vegetables and fruit in our possession?"

"Lift your spell and say my name. All will be taken care of. Farewell, for now Agatha Blackmore. Now, go." He turned and headed back into the wind and snow. Then the old man quickly faded from sight.

"How do we get back to that wall? He led us for miles through the woods. We need to call him back!" Jack ran past me into the snow. "Where is he?"

A horn sounded in the distance. I looked back in the direction we came from; tiny figures could be seen in the distance. "Jack, it's time to go." I pointed at our pursuers.

"Why are they chasing us?" He ran back to me.

"Remember what I told Sims? It's their nature. Come on." We stepped onto the path and into the darkness of the forest. I remember taking two steps into darkness then the bright light of the sun and snapping of cameras woke me.

The two of us stepped out of a wall directly in front of the Richmond Police, the press, and the local FBI Director.

"What the hell!" The locals jumped back in shock from us. I looked down and saw that we resembled snowmen.

"Agent Dalton, is that you?" The local FBI Director peered right at us.

"Director Haskel, are we interrupting something?"

The local covered the microphone in front of him. "Yes, I was about to announce the apprehension of the killer to the press. Thank you for catching him for us."

I began brushing the snow off my bosses jacket and then my own clothing. "What killer would that be, Director?"

"You did a perp walk not twenty minutes ago with a man in costume, where is he by the way?"

Jack looked past the Director at Agent Sims. She was trying to hide behind Haskel. "That was not the killer; that was our guide. We have already solved who killed Chef Lash, and it was not the man in costume. Come on Agent Blackmore we have a report to write." He grabbed my arm and pulled me away from the press conference.

"Dalton come back here!" Agent Dalton let go of my arm. I began to follow him. "Damn you, Dalton!"

"Are you going to tell him what happened?"

"Nope. It's not his jurisdiction. Remember what I told you about this division?"

"So what is he going to tell the reporters?"

"No idea. We need to write everything up and get it sent off to Washington. They are going to want to know about the Fae. What was that King's name?"

"King Dolon of the Dusk Fae is what our guide said his name was." Jack stopped and turned around.

"That's another thing. What was up with the guide? Why did he abandon us like that?"

"Jack, what do you remember about the guide?" I looked into his eyes they almost looked glazed.

"He was the tree guy you found. He led us to those guys dressed like crows. That was some pretty fast talking you did to get up out of there. You were holding out on me Agatha." He turned and headed toward the RV.

As we stepped inside to begin the paperwork, I sat heavily into one of the chairs. Why did Jack not experience what I did? I would have to find time to call Grams and ask. Two Gods have now influenced my life. What did it mean?

"Hey, you're back. Where's my hay? Did you realize you forgot to feed the Unicorn? I'm starving here!"

CHAPTER EIGHT

WRITING the reports out took several hours. Fortunately, the FBI had upgraded the system to mostly digital a few years before I joined. Unfortunately, Magical crimes had not completely.

"That is one of your jobs Agatha. We need to modernize the systems in here, and it is part of your assignment to do so."

"I'm sort of a newbie when it comes to computers and electronics. I mean, I took the classes. But I didn't grow up with it like many children. I was allowed on grandmother's home computer on special occasions, but those were very rare. She taught me to type on an old electric typewriter of mother's."

"No excuses. This is from higher. We need to streamline and modernize. Good work on the Chef case by the way. My boss said we would both be getting commendations. He asked how we popped out of that wall during the press conference?"

"I'm not sure? As I wrote in my report, the Fae sent us through that portal so they must have wanted it to happen. They can be tricksters if they want to."

"Ha ha, well they certainly tricked Haskel. He looked pretty funny standing up there telling the press he was mistaken. Just like I told you in the beginning; don't trust the locals. They are all glory hounds. I'm a little disappointed in Sims and Reynolds for setting us up like that. They both knew your guide wasn't the perp we were looking for."

"What did you tell the locals about Chef Lash's death?"

Jack rubbed his forehead like he had a headache. "Sorry. What was the question?" He was squinting at the paper in his hand.

"Are you OK?"

"I'm fine. Ever since we got back, I've had the worst headache. Ever since I took this job, I've gotten migraines at least once a year. This is the worst one though." He rubbed his head some more. "Your question?"

"Yeah. What did we give the locals and the press about Lash's death?" I considered giving Jack grandmother's headache remedy.

He shook his head. "It came from above for that one. Washington doesn't want to remind the public that the Fae even ever existed. The press was told he was dealing in magical artifacts and was supplied with something that killed him. All the reports state that the man seen being arrested was the one who provided the deadly material."

"That's crazy! Why would a world renowned celebrity do something like this anyway? It sounds like a cover up."

"No one will see the reports we file. From now on anything having to do with the Fae is considered Above Top Secret. Even I can't look into that compartment. Sorry Agatha. It really is a good thing those walk-in coolers were empty when we opened them up. What did you say happened to it all?"

"Magick." His memory loss made me wonder how many times they have zapped him in the past. I wonder if Washington was aware of it?

"Right. Remind me to have you start explaining how that worked later. All knowledge is important. Now we need to get moving."

"Where are we going?"

Handing me a map Jack explained. "We follow a pre-designed route. Washington is our starting place; we travel South to Richmond then down to Charleston, South Carolina. Continuing down, we stop in Jacksonville, Florida. The FBI has a large facility that monitors the Southeast there. Then its Atlanta, Nashville, St Louis, then down again to New Orleans. From there we begin our trek West. We go to Texas by way of Dallas, then over to Oklahoma City and Albuquerque. Continuing on we go to Las Vegas, then San Francisco. It's a giant loop across the country ending back at Washington. You were lucky I was in the area. If not you would have been put on the plane and sent to me."

"We have a plane? Is it like the one in that TV show, the one about the BAU?"

"Not quite, but I think it's pretty cool. If we get a case further away than we can drive, they will send it to us. You'll see."

"How many times have you made the loop?"

Jack cocked his head and thought. "Not counting airplane hops and once by train, I think it's about ten times. We get diverted a lot. Some cases have taken months to finish. Every time we have a rogue hunt they send for us."

"You mentioned that before. What is a rogue hunt?'

"Were creatures or a rare Vampire that has either killed or broken the law in some way. They usually run for it. Almost always actually. The Weres figure they can shift and hide somewhere. The Vamps don't want to die or be imprisoned. If they don't kill themselves, others do it for them. Currently, there is only one Vampire in Federal Custody."

"I didn't know that. Why do we have one locked up?"

"His name is Charles Maddox. He and his coven were arrested after they killed a movie star in the late 1960s. The coven were all killed in the police stand-off, but Charlie surrendered to police. He really thought we would turn him over to the local nest for trial by his elders."

"What happened? Did they refuse to try him?"

"None of the locals responded to our requests to take him. A special prison had to be set up in California to hold him. He is serving life without parole. His case is one of the reasons we have so few Vampire attacks. The elders that are in this country have proclaimed there are to be no more spectacles. His trial was a real doozy. Look it up online if you get a chance. Think of it as a homework assignment if you like. Maybe you can tell me what we did wrong Magically. It surprises me that they didn't teach about him in school. I'll have to send your Director a note about that."

"Has he ever tried to escape?"

"Not to my knowledge. Some of his fellow prisoners have tried to kill him a few times. They said he told them to do it. He comes up for parole every few years, and they shoot down any of the requests."

"Why not just give him the death penalty and be done with it?"

"California is a non-death state, remember? He would have to commit a crime outside the state. His trial and ordeal are the reasons we use Vampire enforcers in any related investigation. They are authorized for termination." He shook his head. "I've only been on two Vamp hunts since taking this job. They're pretty rare."

"Do you work with enforcers from all the paranormals?"

Giving me a funny look; Jack asked. "What do you mean all the paranormals? I know of the Vampires and those on the Were reservations, but there are more?"

"Of course there are. We police our own; I thought you knew that? How can the FBI have a Magical crimes division and not know any of this stuff?"

"To be truthful, we don't run into very much of it. Most magical crimes take place under the radar. It's exposure to technology that is bringing so much to light. Under the old systems, reports got lost or were changed to exclude that information. Now it's instantaneous. Since we went digital completely, I've been busier than I have ever been. When Washington told me I had a chance to get you I was excited. Maybe we can catch some of those that have escaped our notice and stop them."

Jack stood and began pulling books and things from one of the many cabinets that lined the interior walls. "Take these. They are case studies and reports from some of the higher profile cases this office has done." He pulled down a large box. "This is all the manuals and catalogs for equipment for an RV like this. We can get the easy stuff from most vendors and have local companies install it. This is your long term project. Now let's get closed up and get out of here. Roads to find and crimes to stop."

I jumped up and grabbed my new more complete checklist. I had added a few things to it that he forgot about. Number one was checking on Fergus and make sure he is where he is supposed to be.

Conveniently there is a handle on top of his barn, I grabbed it and moved him to the kitchen counter.

"Hey! Why am I rattling around like a rubber ball in here?"

"Sorry Fergus but it's time to go. I'm just putting you in a safe place while we close the slides." I locked the barn in place with Velcro strips I had on the counter.

"Tell me when you move me next time! I was grooming Desirae, and now she's all dirty again."

I just had to know. I opened the roof of the barn and looked inside. "Who is Desirae?"

"Hey! I'm naked in here!" Fergus was standing in one of the stalls with a plastic toy horse. The horse was purple and had screaming red hair.

"How did you redecorate the barn?" The walls no longer had pictures of cartoon farm animals on them. Some of the world's ugliest wallpaper now lined the walls. Gone were the barn fixtures and doll house furniture now stood in its place. Only the toy horse had a stall. Fergus had a toy bed covered in hay upstairs in the loft.

"I have resources."

"Did Chuck help you with all this?"

"You don't like it? I did it for Desirae."

"Didn't Cat give her to you?" It looked a bit like one of the ponies off the TV show he liked.

"I have no idea what you are talking about."

I was about to say something more, but Jack began yelling about moving on.

"We will discuss this later. Hold on to your hay!" I hit the button for the slides, and the RV began to shake as they slid closed. I ran outside to pull the chucks and make sure we weren't connected to anything.

"Jack we're good to go!" I jumped back into my chair and put on my seat belt. Jack wasn't a bad driver, but he wasn't used to having breakables on board. Namely me!

It was a bit strange to be traveling with a man I barely knew. We were both Agents and he was my boss, but I knew very little about him. The Director had told me to trust him. On one of my free days on the road I sent a text to Anastasia the tech supervisor I met last year. She gave me the lowdown on Agent Jack Dalton.

Jack was married! He hadn't said anything to me yet, but his wife lived outside of Dallas. His job kept him away from her, but he always made it a point to spend time when he was in the area. According to Anastasia he had been in this truck for years. He was too good at his job to allow him to leave it. She gave him a pretty good reference. She told me Chuck said 'Hi.'

The camper bunk bed was not the most comfortable bed I had ever slept in, but the new mattress helped. Each bunk had a small TV, lamp, and very small bookcase. The privacy curtain could close, and there was a way to secure it. For the first week on board, I set a ward at night just to be sure. I discovered that my boss had his own facilities at the back in his room, so the very small bathroom was all mine to use. Not being an early riser we evolved a sort of system for mornings and meals.

I was sitting in my usual spot staring at the sun. "Good morning Agatha."

"Good morning to you too, Jack." I smiled. His idea of breakfast was drinking a nasty cup of coffee every morning.

"You were up earlier than usual today."

"It's almost Samhain. I was doing a few rituals and blessing my spell components. Do we have more work this time of year?"

"Samhain? Oh, you mean Halloween. We do as a matter of fact. All the offices do. It's the one time a year that most Agents ever encounter Magical or paranormal crimes in their districts. They will generally only call us if it's a big one or something unusual. The regular crimes are enough for most offices."

"Back home this is usually a time for celebration. They decorate the whole town, and people come for miles to visit our Harvest fair."

"I read about your town in the file Madelaine sent me. Are purple squirrels really that big of a draw?"

I covered my eyes. Those things would haunt me my whole life. "Yes. I never meant for that to happen you know. I was four. Now I've gone and done it again. Quantico won't ever forget me now."

"It won't be that bad. How many of those are there?"

"Thousands by now. I'll be lucky if the FBI keeps me on after this assignment. Most regular spells I can do. It's only ones that involve living creatures or weather that I seem to screw up."

"Weather?"

"That wasn't in my file? I accidentally made fog come out of a statue last year."

"I don't remember seeing that in there. Why would fog be a big deal?"

"It wouldn't, but it didn't stop. They had to change the name of the park from pumpkin square to eternal fog."

Jack started laughing. "You know I have to find that report now, don't you?"

I nodded. "What are our plans for the day?"

"Direction change. The reason I was up so early was I got our new assignment. We need to get to Warner Robbins Air Base as soon as possible."

"Why there?"

"Well, that is where the plane is landing for us. We have a case, but it's in San Diego. There has been a magical theft of a very valuable necklace."

"Why call us? Isn't that something more for the locals?"

"Good. You're learning. Yes, normally. However, this is very high profile. The locals are completely stumped, and my boss wants us there. He thinks between the two of us we can figure it out and make the Bureau look good."

"Who does it belong to?"

"The movie Goddess herself, Marilyn Kelly. The missing piece was taken from a special exhibition of her career at the film actor's guild. It was literally a locked room theft."

"Those happen all the time. Safes are pretty easy for thieves to break into."

"Yes, they are. But this was in a magic-proof box on a pedestal in a locked and secured room in sight of cameras and two armed guards. Yes, we searched the guards."

"Let's get moving then. I can't wait to fly!"

He smiled at me. "Let me grab a bite to eat, and we'll get moving."

CHAPTER NINE

"THIS PLANE IS TERRIBLE!" We hit another pocket of turbulence that bounced me around the seat I was strapped to. I looked over at Jack and he was sound asleep! Oof! My head flew back and bounced off the hard wall of the plane. I reached back to rub my head and looked around for the hundredth time. All I could think about was how excited I had been, and how funny Jack thought my reaction was when I first saw the plane.

"What is that? That's not our plane is it?" I stared in horror at the large, green aircraft.

Jack smiled at me. "It is. That is a C-17 Globemaster. It will be taking us and the RV to San Diego."

"How? There is no way this big thing can fit inside there." I peered out the window at the enormous plane.

"It will be pretty close, but the RV will just fit. They have a bigger plane, the C-5, but none are at the base right now. Don't worry it's safe." He drove right up to the back of the plane. As I watched, the back of the plane opened right up with a big ramp extending down.

"That doesn't look very big."

"I talked to one of the pilots; they carry helicopters all the time inside one of these. We had a visiting Australian pilot once, and he said they put a semi-truck loaded with a submarine in one of theirs. That I would have liked to see!"

As we watched, crew members came out and began laying smaller wooden ramps at the end of the larger metallic ramps. Jack said this was so that the RV was level as it entered the plane. The height of the opening inside was a little over twelve feet. Our RV was ten feet plus in some spots. It was going to be close.

Jack and I were not allowed to ride inside the RV for the trip, so I grabbed a protesting Fergus and left the vehicle.

"Why do I have to get out? I was all comfortable in the barn."

"If I have to get out so do you. It's called teamwork."

"I want a new team! What the hell is this thing? We are taking the truck with us, into a plane? If Unicorns were meant to fly, they would have given us wings! Who can I protest this to?"

I shoved his little protesting ass into my pocket. Looking at Jack, I smiled. "He can be annoying sometimes."

"I didn't notice."

"Sure you didn't." As I watched, the loadmaster carefully loaded the RV onto the airplane. They very slowly backed it up the slight incline ramp.

"Come on; they won't wait too much longer for us." Jack waved me forward.

One of the crew met me at the ramp. She was wearing khaki pants with a tee shirt. Sweat poured down her face and as she hopped down. The hot Georgia sun made the concrete extremely hot. "First time on one of these?"

"Yes. Does it show?" That gained me a smile.

"We have to strap the truck down so it doesn't roll around or shift as we fly. You and the other Agent get to ride up toward the front of the aircraft. Loading your truck sure beats transporting helicopters into the desert." She had to shout because the plane's engines made a loud rumbling noise.

"How big is this thing?" It was sort of like a big metallic tunnel.

"We have eighty-eight feet of cargo space. The hold is eighteen feet wide and twelve feet high. Your RV is almost too tall, so we have it at the tallest spot of the aircraft. We can lift one hundred and seventy thousand pounds. Just yesterday we flew a tank across the country."

"That's crazy! I'm surprised to see a woman doing all this stuff."

"Thanks! I love it. We have lots of women crew-members, it's the new military." I could hear the sarcasm in her tone.

"I'm sorry if you took me the wrong way. I grew up in a small secluded town, a lot of this is new to me. Joining the FBI was a real eye-opener let me tell you. I think it's great that women are in the military! We can do just about anything a man can do."

"What do you do in the FBI, you look pretty young?"

"I get that. I just started my internship for my fourth year at the Academy. I'm an investigative Agent due to being a Witch."

"No way! Really?" She looked me over.

"I left my pointy hat in the truck. Just kidding!" The look on her face! "Seriously, though, I'm the first Witch to be accepted at the Bureau."

"We have a few Weres around here, but you are the first real Witch I've ever met. I've seen some of those Russian mercs, but we don't see them on our planes."

"I'm better than those guys." She walked me past the RV. The walls were metal covered in heavy plastic in places. There were fire extinguishers everywhere. The seats she showed me folded down from the walls.

"This is where you and the other Agent will sit. Do you need to use the head? Once we leave you will have to hold it." She handed me some hearing protection and told me it would be very noisy.

I told her I went on the RV. She showed me how to use the five-point seat belt and made sure I was secure. Jack trotted up while I was getting comfortable and strapped himself in. The engines started to whine louder as the ramp in back started to close up.

"Here we go!" Jack leaned back in his seat and closed his eyes.

The roaring became thunderous, and I felt a lurch as the wheels started to move. The woman who helped me was strapped down into her seat across from us alongside the rest of the crew. I assumed the pilots had their own compartments. I made a mental note to try and get a look once we got to California. The rumbling of the tires on the runway could really be felt now as the plane shook and jumped a bit. I felt my connection to the element of Earth disappear as we left the ground. I concentrated on Air and said a prayer to Aeolus. He ruled the winds.

"Are you OK?" I looked up, and Jack was peering at me.

"I'm OK. Just saying a prayer." He nodded like he understood.

I smiled at the plane's crew as they pulled out tablets or ebook readers. I left mine in the truck so I tried to meditate. Nudging Jack I asked how long this flight would take.

"Just shy of five hours. It's right at two thousand miles away. This plane can fly almost three thousand miles without stopping. If we had to drive, it would have taken at least two days. It's about thirty-five hours straight through, but almost double that in an RV. I'm going to take a nap. Wake me up if you need something." He pulled out a hat and covered his face with it.

I went back to my meditation. This last case left a lot of unanswered questions. Why are the Gods interested in me? This was twice now that I have experienced a physical meeting of a God form. I barely remember Hekate's visit, but Cat saw her too, so it did happen. The fact that Jack didn't remember the same experience as I did was troubling. There was no way he could not have encountered the Fae in all this time of investigating Magical Crimes. They were experts in mischief and taking both people and things that they like. The whole thing reminded me of one of my favorite movies. Did 'Men in Black' actually exist? It would make sense that he was flashy-thing zapped more than once. Or at least the Fae version of it. Our superiors knew of the Fae why not Jack?

I meditated on the facts I knew for a couple of hours. When I opened my eyes, Jack was awake and reading from a file. He nudged me and handed it to me. "This is the background I received for the new case. Make sure you familiarize yourself with it."

I took the file and began to read.

Marilyn Kelly, known as the 'Goddess of Film' began her career in the late 1940s. She first appeared as a waitress in 'It's a wonderful life' and then began co-starring with many of the great actors of our time. Transitioning into the 1950s, she headlined on the strength of her own acting. By the 1960s, questions began to arise as she seemed never to age. Her age has never been stated officially. Modern bloggers and film historians have pointed out Pre-Demon War films from Germany of an actress that resembled her. Miss Kelly has neither confirmed nor denied she was that actress. She seemed to age just a bit in the 1970s, leaving the young girl look behind, but she even now looks to be in her thirties.

Official government records show her immigration to the US in 1945 from France. Her stated date of birth on her passport was 1925. Other than tax records, very little officially is known about her. It has been suspected that she is a crossbreed of Fae, Witch, or Were.. She has been seen in daylight and coming from Europe precludes her being a Vampire.

I stared at the pictures in the file. She looked really good for a woman over a hundred years old. Witches lived a long time, but I had never heard of her being one of us. If she was Were, she would have to shift at least once a month. She could be a non-shifting Were. That can happen when paranormals marry mundanes. She drives cars and lives in a modern city, so Fae is out of the question. I shifted my thoughts to the actual case.

The necklace in question was made of gold. Rubies, diamonds, moonstone, and sapphires made up the basic pattern. A jade turtle motif hung in the center. Something sparked in the back of my brain about that combination of gems, but I shelved it for now. I would study that later. According to the report, the necklace was a family heirloom. She loaned the necklace out to the San Diego Natural

History Museum for a special exhibition of jewels through the ages. A special display case purchased by the actress was to be used. According to the local investigators, only magic could have removed it. I closed the file and handed it back to Jack.

"What is your first impression, Agatha?"

"Definitely a magical crime. Does she have any enemies?"

"Good question. She claims not. But we still don't know how she has lived this long or stayed so young. By the way if you should discover that secret you are to report it."

"Why do they wish to know?"

"I share your suspicions, but I don't think it's nefarious in any way. While we are aware of many of the paranormal races, there are some we know nothing about. This is one of those requests I think."

I nodded but wasn't so sure about that order.

"I would have to see the crime scene to detect more."

"So would I. It's a classic locked room crime. I told the local office to preserve the scene as much as possible. Remember what you learned on the last case. Don't trust the locals and be careful how much you give away information wise." He looked at his watch. "We should be on the ground in less than an hour."

I nodded my agreement and began analyzing what I knew. This should be a fun one.

———

THE PLANE LANDED with no real notice other than the roar of the engines. As we came to a rumbling stop, I checked on Fergus. The little devil was sound asleep in my pocket.

I watched as the plane's crew unloaded the RV. It was faster getting it off than putting it on. I thanked the crew and did a quick walk around just to make sure we weren't damaged in any way.

"Where are we?" I asked Jack as I climbed on board.

"This is Marine Corps Air Station Miramar. You might have seen a movie about this place. They do the Top Gun competitions out here or at least they used to. I'm not up on my Air Force statistics. I was a Marine in my former life."

"You were? That's cool. I guess the transition to FBI Agent was pretty easy then."

He nodded. "Some. I was a Marine Police Officer. My primary duties involved Intelligence operations. My wife wanted me to do something more US based. When I got out, I applied to the other Academy for training."

"Where is that one located at?" I knew the FBI had a school for older Agent recruits just not where it was.

"It is at Camp Pendleton where the Marines train on this side of the country. The training is a bit less education based and more hands on. To qualify you need to be at least twenty-three years old and a US citizen. They want you to have three years minimum law enforcement experience along with a college education."

"Grandmother wanted me to do that program initially. It was only after an Agent came to the house that I went to Quantico."

"Right. The regular training used to be done at Quantico until the Demon War after-effects happened. Too many paranormals wanted to join, hence the school you went to. To join as an older Agent there are a lot of tests and picky qualifications to meet. We tend to be very strict about selecting the right sort of Agents." As we talked, Jack navigated through the base and out onto the streets of San Diego.

"The History Museum is in Balboa Park along with the Zoo and other places. Traffic shouldn't be too bad. They are expecting us."

The city was different than those on the East coast. More palm trees and sort of a Spanish look to many of the houses. Balboa Park was huge. I caught a glimpse of signs for the zoo as we went past.

"If we have time we can do a rest day here. You could at least hit the zoo and maybe the art museum. I hear it's really nice. But we have to solve the case first."

I smiled at him thinking that would be great. Jack pulled the RV around the back of a huge white building with a glass peaked roof.

Several local police and suit-clad Agents stood on the loading dock as we backed in.

"Remember stay professional and give them as little information as possible. This is more their case than ours."

"Gotcha." I grabbed my spell bag and checked my tools over.

We stepped out together and approached the Agent on the dock.

"Hello, Jack. Come to take all the glory?"

"Washington sent us here. Not my choice, Jacob. This is Agent Blackmore; she's interning with me this year."

"A little young for your style of job isn't she?"

"She is a good addition to the team. Have your people found anything more about the theft?"

"Always to the point with you. That would be no. Not a damn thing. That necklace might as well have never existed for all the traces left." I perked up at what he said. An Illusion spell might be the answer.

"You might as well take a look." He motioned for us to follow him.

We followed the Agent past towering dinosaurs and a few paranormal monsters that stood on the main floor. I saw a stuffed Unicorn on display and made a note not to come back this way with Fergus. I would never hear the end of it from him. Overhead flew winged reptiles including a very lifelike dragon. Grandmother had quite a few tales about those creatures. I was surprised to see one here though. They were very rare and thinking sentient creatures. The theft had occurred in the new wing devoted to gemstones and their historical uses. I took one last look at the dragon. If the dragon had been a real one, it would have been a good choice for who or what took the necklace. Dragons treasured all things shiny and valuable.

Police officers stood at the entrance to the wing. We took a moment to sign in to the scene and slip on some booties. Better to not contaminate anything. Techs were still printing and processing the entire hall and exhibits.

"This is where the guards were positioned. Miss Kelly had a

contract with the Museum that living guards, as well as cameras, were to watch her property 24/7 as long it was here. We questioned them extensively and released them. The video record shows the necklace just vanishing from the case all on its own."

Jack glanced at me and gave me a get to work look. "I will need to see the video records along with any interviews you did. Agent Blackmore is a Witch. She is going to cast a few diagnostic spells and start figuring out what we are dealing with here."

"She's a Witch? One recognized by the Council?" The local agent looked in my direction as I started looking around the room.

"Yes. Our first Official Witch Agent. Now about those tapes..." The other Agent led Jack off to; I assumed, the security office.

Slipping into my magical scan meditation, I stared at the room. Magick was everywhere! The exhibit was titled Gemstones through the Ages. Ancient Egyptian and Greek jewelry settings were some of the first displayed. They thrummed with Magickal potential. I peered at them closer. Pulling out my investigative camera, I snapped a few pictures. The cards explaining their use was all wrong. Sometime in their history a high priestess owned them. The Magick had a female vibe to it.

I moved on down the line. Various unset gems and crystals gave off different power vibrations. I wondered if the museum had hired someone to ward the room? I would have to check. If they didn't, the room could use something. This modern section contained items from a wide selection of the rich and famous. Small spells that enhanced glamour, health, wealth, and longevity simply covered the jewelry. Looking at who provided it I could see why. Most celebrities have some sort of vanity they wished to enhance. Only someone with a Magickal background could see them. The Magick led me to the case belonging to our actress.

Her case also thrummed with power. An item of great power had been here once. I was surprised she allowed it to be separated from her person if it was this powerful. Didn't she know? Security spells were inlaid all over the case. I could sense anti-theft, and tracers build into the Plexiglas. That intrigued me. Magickal trace filled the air; something was here, and something took the necklace, but I couldn't figure what that was.

"Did you find anything?" I glanced up and saw the local Agent Jacob.

"Yes and no. Many of these other pieces have spells on them. This case has them built into both the plexi and the stand. Do you know who built it?"

The Agent pulled out his tablet and began scrolling through it. "Miss Kelly provided the display, but she said that..." He looked at me and smiled. "Sorry Agent Blackmore but I will keep this lead to myself." He grabbed one of the wandering Agents, and they practically ran from the room.

"False lead or mistake?"

I looked over at Jack who was watching me. "Both? This case is fascinating, but I doubt the one who created it is our thief. Something like this is very expensive to both make and buy. The craftsmanship is what interested me."

"Good. Jacob needs a wild goose chase to go after. We worked together a few years ago in Atlanta. He and his boss took all the credit for a zombie hunt I conducted a few years ago."

"Necromancer?"

"Yes. How did you know?"

"That's a really rare power. I have heard of a spell that makes Zombies, but grandmother said only a Necromancer could truly make the dead follow them."

"It was pretty bad. The local Witches Council sent their Enforcers after the rogue. I only assisted in locating him. They did all the heavy lifting." He glanced around at the room. None of the techs were anywhere around us. "What did you find out?"

"Half the stuff in this room has a Magickal vibe to it. The missing necklace must have some really powerful spells on it because some of this stuff is powerful on its own. Those first two Greek and Egyptian displays would have stopped my grandmother in her tracks."

"That bad?"

"Yup. Did you see the Unicorn and Dragon in the main hall? It makes me wonder what else is in here? Lots of Magick in the air. Do we get to meet Miss Kelly? I'd like to ask her a few questions."

"She lives local so I can inquire. Good work."

I wandered out into the main hall. Magickal traces were out here too. The Unicorn was a real one. Information on the card said it had been a stallion from the zoo at the turn of the century. The exhibit made mention to visit the others there. I made a note to ask Fergus if he wished to visit other Unicorns. Mixed in with the Dinosaurs were a few other paranormal creatures such as a Chupacabra and Bigfoot. I squinted at the Bigfoot display. Those were definitely an intelligent species!

"Can I help you, Miss?" I turned to see one of the Museum Docents.

"Yes. The Bigfoot display. Bigfoot is an intelligent species. Are those real?"

The Docent looked at me funny. "What do you mean by real?"

"Are those stuffed Bigfoot or just a display?"

"That is something I have never been asked before. Let me call for one of the curators." He pulled out a radio and muttered a few words into it. "It will be a few moments. The theft in the mineral wing has everyone on edge."

After a few minutes, a short man in a white lab smock hurried over followed by one of the Museum security guards. I rolled my eyes at that. This should be fun.

"Is there a problem here?" The guard carefully stepped past the curator and circled around behind me.

"Yes, sir. This young lady wants to know about the Bigfoot display. She asked if they were real or just a display? I have never been asked something like that before."

"The large one is a stuffed example taken by a hunter in 1956 in Oregon. The rest are mock-ups."

"Are you aware that Bigfoot is an Intelligent Paranormal Species? It is my understanding they have a treaty with the US government."

The man's eyes widened a bit. "Um, I think you are mistaken about that young lady. Our studies have shown that they are a form of ape native to this continent."

"That may be, but they were participants in the 1915 Interspecies Treaty with the US. They signed the treaty."

This shook up the white coat a bit, and he made a motion to the guard who laid a hand on me. "OK Miss it's time for you to go."

"I think not." I motioned with my hand, and he froze in midspeech. "Now, my name is Agent Agatha Blackwood with FBI Magical Crimes. Nobody touches the Witch."

CHAPTER TEN

"AGATHA, IS THERE A PROBLEM HERE?" I shook my arm free of the now frozen security guard and turned to Jack.

"Not anymore. I was just explaining to this person that Bigfoot is an Intelligent Species that signed the Interspecies 1915 treaty with the US. He told me that," I pointed to the exhibit, "over there is a stuffed Bigfoot killed in the 1950s. That is a murder victim on display."

Jack visibly winced. He looked at the frozen guard and nodded at him.

"Oops. Sorry." I waved, and the guard shook his head and reached for me again. "If you grab me again I will do something worse than just freeze you!" A ball of flame materialized in my hand.

The guard pulled back in shock and reached for his gun. Jack held up his badge and spoke to the now panicked man.

"She is an FBI Agent. Stop! Agatha, stand down please."

I let the ball of flame disappear. "She's correct about the treaty and the exhibit. We are here investigating the theft, but this just got added to our case. I suggest you call someone higher than you. Unless you want me to arrest you?"

The surprised curator paled and nearly bolted. The docent grabbed his radio and called for more help. Jack gave me the eye. I was going to hear about the fireball later I was sure.

"Let's move this somewhere less public shall we?" Jack was eying the civilians starting to take notice of our conversation. The guard snapped out of his shock and suggested one of the conference rooms. One of the Museum managers and his legal council showed up just as we all found the room.

"What is the meaning of this?" The manager was a beefy looking man in an expensive looking suit.

"Which part?" Jack held out his hand to the manager. "I'm Special Agent Jack Dalton, Magical Crimes unit. My partner and I are here about the theft, but Agent Blackmore noticed a crime in your Museum."

"What crime?"

"She asked these gentlemen about the Bigfoot exhibit. Instead of answering her questions they tried to have her removed, not knowing she is FBI. Were you aware the Bigfoot is an Intelligent Species and a signatory to the 1915 Interspecies Accords?"

The man froze in mid-tirade as Jack's words hit home. The legal council started to defend his boss.

"That is outrageous. We have had that exhibit in this museum for over fifty years!"

"So you admit that you knowingly had a murder victim on exhibit in your museum?"

"Wait, what?" The lawyer paled and began to stutter.

"That is why we asked you down. That display is of a murder, as I'm assuming any other Bigfoot bodies you have in storage are also. Why else show a family unit?"

"We had no idea! It doesn't say that on the document!"

I pulled up the original document off the Internet. I knew it was in there because that was one thing grandmother made me memorize before leaving home. 'Always know your rights.' One of her favorite sayings. I brought up the list of species and the signature line.

"It's right here in the public record." I pointed the line out to the men. "Unicorns were almost added, but they had no speaking language at the time. This needs to be updated as more paranormals have come forward since then. But as a matter of law, it says Bigfoot right there." I handed the tablet to the lawyer who took it from me with shaky hands.

The research curator came over and looked at the tablet too. I saw him pale for just a moment. "What else do you have in this museum?"

I mentally ran through the list thinking what a mundane would consider a beast. The only non-human on the list were the Thunderbirds. Only one showed up at the conference, and I think the Fae translated for them at the time.

"There is a Thunderbird here somewhere isn't there?" The Manager paled even further.

"Don't answer her." The lawyer perked up and tried to protect the museum.

Jack turned toward the two suits. "Covering up a murder or hiding a body is a Federal offense." The security guard had his radio in his hand was about to broadcast when Jack looked at him. "Try and cover something up and I'll throw you under the jail. Agatha call Jacob or one of his minions in here, please. We will let the locals in on this; we still have to go interview Miss Kelly."

I ran back the mineral room and grabbed the first local Agent I could find. The man jumped as I grabbed him, but the prospect of a double murder broke him from his surprise.

"You needed my assistance Special Agent Dillon?" The Agent was practically begging for an assignment. Jack filled him in on what I had discovered, and he jumped right in.

Jack nodded to me, and we exited the room. "Good work Agatha! Not our immediate case but sharp eyes. Heads will roll over that one to be sure. I'm surprised no one reported it sooner."

"My people have a tendency to stay away from these sort of places. Too many burial grounds and cultural misappropriation happens in here. I have nothing against bone-pickers but they need to respect our culture rather than make stuff up about it."

"That sounds like the voice of experience." Jack pulled me away, and we started walking.

"We had a visit from a local Boston college that wanted to 'study' New England Witch culture and thought our town was the best place to do that." I glanced at Jack and could see he was listening.

"What did they do?"

"They followed Grandmother around for about a week hiding behind trees and filming her without her permission. They then requested permission from the town council to study the graveyards and local celebratory events."

"I hear an oops coming up."

"Pretty much. They didn't do their research and Grandmother is on the council. She denied their request and hexed the cameras they were using. Since it was the equivalent of saying no to being filmed, the local Sheriff laughed them out of his office. They then broke the law by trying to excavate a grave-site on property they rented from a local mundane."

"I assume they were arrested?" We were heading back to the RV to go visit Miss Kelly.

"Oh, yeah. Cappy, our police chief, called the State police just to make sure the charges stuck. We did get an apology letter from the college, but we declined dropping the charges."

"Good for you." Jack fiddled with the door.

"Yeah. Can't fix stupid sometimes no matter how much money you throw at it." I followed him into the RV.

We left the museum and headed back toward the harbor. As we left the park, several Black Government Suburbans passed us with lights flashing.

"Looks like Jacob is on his way back."

"That was nice of you to give him that case."

"It was smart. He will stay out from underfoot while we do our jobs. It's the perfect distraction for him." As we drove into the city proper, I remarked on how many of the houses looked the same.

"Haven't you been in cities before?"

"Just a few. I seldom left our little town. Many of the people in town were afraid of me. My magic gets a tiny bit out of control at times and things happen. The worst thing I ever did was change Camila into a chicken."

"Really?"

"It was just for about five minutes. I changed her back. She has been afraid of me since I made the purple squirrels. It was an accident. She may be my Aunt, but she is a nasty woman. I was visiting my mother at the hospital and she intruded. It was the first time I had seen her in almost ten years. Grandmother took me in because Camilla refused. She started yelling that I wasn't supposed to be there and I just lost it."

"That is not in your file."

"Grandmother helped me to focus my magic and I changed her back. She was a pink chicken for only a few minutes, but that was enough for her. As soon as I was old enough, she started to petition the town to make me leave. The FBI saved me from exile."

"Why did you need help focusing? Couldn't your grandmother do the spell?"

"She could, but it wouldn't have worked. Only those that cast the spell can take it off. If I had been younger or confused, she might still be a pink fowl. I use it as a threat all the time now. Not that I can go home anytime soon. Once I'm a full Agent, I will have neutral status, and they can't stop me from visiting."

"It's good to have goals."

"It is. The map says to turn right at the light." We had been following the computer directions.

The road wound around the coastal area ending at a huge iron gate. A large house stood on the cliff overlooking the harbor area. We stopped at the gate and rang the bell.

"What do you want?" The speaker was a man's voice.

"Agent's Dalton and Blackmore to see Miss Kelly about the theft at the museum."

There was silence for a few moments. "Drive up the road to the house and park in front. Someone will meet you at the door." The gate began to open.

"Nice folks."

"Yeah. Wonderful. This should be interesting." More details about the house could be seen as we approached it. It was an Italian villa style with large windows and stucco exterior. It was at least three stories with balconies and iron railings. She definitely wasn't a Fae with that much cold iron around. Of course, it could be a deterrent too. The driveway became a circle around a large fountain. Jack parked the RV.

"Like always, bring anything you might need."

I nodded. I was starting to build a routine for every case.

A man in a butler uniform waited for us by the front door.

"Agents Dalton and Blackmore to see Miss Kelly?"

"Of course." He opened the door for us to go inside and followed us in.

"Miss Kelly is out by the pool. If you would follow me please?" He led us through the palatial house. The furnishing was of a European style almost a century out of date. The back of the house overlooked the ocean. The view was awesome, what we could see of it. The pool area dominated the entire rear. You could play water polo in that pool it was so big. I thought California was having a water shortage?

"What can I do for you Agents?" The voice came from under an umbrella in front of us. We stepped forward just a bit and could see a woman sitting in the shade wearing a very skimpy bikini and sunglasses.

I let Jack take the lead on this one. "Miss Kelly we came to ask you a few questions about your necklace."

"Of course. Would you like to sit?" She waved at the butler who brought over a pair of chairs.

"Thank you." We sat and stared into the shade at the actress many called an 'eternal goddess' of screen and film.

"What would you like to know?"

"I understand your necklace was taken on the last day of the exhibit. Have you ever displayed it before publicly?"

"I have. There was a similar display at the same museum in 1975 that I placed it in. They asked, and I allowed it for only one weekend just like this time."

"Why only a weekend?"

"It has been in my family for a very long time. Of all the things that money can buy, it is the one thing I own that is irreplaceable. Do you have any leads on it?"

"We can't really talk about an open case, even to you Miss Kelly. We represent Magical Crimes for the FBI. We will do everything in our power to find it. Do you have any rabid fans or enemies who would take it?"

She pulled her sunglasses down away from her eyes. I could see even in this low light they were a deep blue color. "Max, my butler can give you the list of fans my people have compiled. Enemies are something that I have very few of Agents. When I was younger I had a few, but they should be long gone by now." She straightened her glasses.

"Can you give us any specifics?" Jack stared at her his eyes not leaving her face.

"Can I trust you not to share anything I tell you? I ask because I like both my privacy and my secrets."

"You can trust us. If something leaks, it won't come from the two of us. Higher than us? I can't say."

The actress leaned back in her chair and clasped her hands together. She rested her chin upon her joined hands and thought for a long moment. She let out a sigh. "Trust is so hard for those in the entertainment business. I suppose I can trust you with a few things."

She stared at Jack and smiled tossing a towel over herself and leaning forward.

"My little game didn't work. Sorry Agent Dalton, I play that one with most men."

"I have a wife I love very much. I try not to mix business with pleasure it can lead down the wrong roads in my business."

"Understood. I was in Germany before the Demon Wars. Several of my former lovers and jilted co-workers were in government service. One such man was Dietrich Eckart. He was very high up in the party and was rumored to have the ear of the great leader. I have always assumed he died in the fall of the Empire or was possibly consumed by the Demon as many of the inner circle were. If he lived, he would be well over a hundred as he was born in the late 1800s. He was human but had many contacts in the esoteric communities of the time. If anyone had survived, it would have been him. Only one other person comes to mind that would consider me an enemy or rival enough to steal from me."

"Who is that?"

She let out a sigh. "A woman. Rayne Snow was her name. We were lovers at one point, but she broke it off. She was a Witch and couldn't stay with me for many reasons. I tried to ruin her financially after the breakup. I was the jilted lover, and I paid for it. I'm not saying she hexed me, but my luck in the 1960s was not great. She went by several other names using Frost or Ice as her last name. It was all variations of Snow or Winter. She wasn't very old when we were together so she should be alive."

"She is." I blurted it out. They both looked at me. "Sorry. She goes by Ray Winter now. I know because she's on the American Witches Council."

"Good for her. She always wanted to reach the pinnacle of her craft. If you see her, tell her I'm sorry."

"Anyone else?"

"Not really. Max and his family have been with me since Germany, so it won't be him. I have had a few hack producers or agents over the years, but none of them would have the guts even to try. Max can give you a list."

"Why did you only allow the necklace in the exhibit for only a few days?" Something sounded off.

"As I said it is precious to me. The last time it was a very popular show. I was asked by their board of directors, so I said yes. It was only supposed to be for two days. I miss it already."

"We understand. Is there anything else we should know about it?"

"Not that I can think of. Please find it."

"We will do the best we can Miss Kelly." Jack stood and took her hand. She stood and stepped out into the sun. Still covered with the towel she looked very much like her pictures if maybe a little older. The reports all said she looked to be in her early thirties, but to me, she looked forty like my aunt. Just the slightest bit of gray touched her bangs.

The butler, Max, was waiting for us by the door. "Here are the lists she said for you to have. The larger one is some of her more rabid fans including those that have tried to jump the fence."

"Thank you." We followed him back through the house to the RV.

As we prepared to leave, I looked at Jack. "Did she look older to you?"

"How so?"

"The pictures in the file are only a few months old, but she looks older than that."

"Most likely they have been touched up, or she was in makeup. Anyone on those lists leap out at you?"

"No. It looks like a bunch of nuts. There are attached local police reports for some of them. Max seems to take pretty good care of her."

"How well do you know the councilwoman?"

"Not at all. They are the boogieman in my world. For some reason, they fear Grandmother, so I can ask her about Winter if you like."

"Send her a text and ask. Where is their headquarters?"

"No idea. Not something they spread around. I will send Grand-mother a text right now." I pulled out my cell and typed out a message. "Do you want me to research those Germans?"

"The Thule society? They were the ones behind the Dictator and the Demon Wars. Go ahead and use our files and database for that. We have run into the name of the organization before so some of the information should be in there." I got out of my seat and staggered to the computer station. I sat back down and put on the seat belt.

I typed in Thule first and got several pages of Top Secret documents that I was not authorized to see. I typed in the name Dietrich Eckart, and the records said he was killed in Berlin at the end of the war. Just on a whim, I punched in Rayne Snow. More blacked out documents showed up along with a Top Secret screen. I relayed what I found to Jack as he drove.

"I figured as much. I'll access those areas later and tell you if I find anything useful. Go ahead and start running the list of crazies just in case. I'm heading to the local office here in town. My boss will want a report, but I need to use a secure land line."

I told him OK and started running the records. Lots of nuts in San Diego it seems. Most of these people fell into that category except one.

"Jack one of these looks promising."

"Which one?" He stopped the RV in front of a large glass and brick office. The windows had to be at least four stories high.

"Ernest Bass. He's the janitor at the Museum. He tried breaking into Miss Kelly's gate one night five years ago. He was arrested for breaking and entering also weapons charges."

"What weapons?"

"He claimed she was a Vampire and tried to get in to finish her according to his statement. He was sentenced to three years. He had a stake gun he made from PVC pipe and an aerosol can. He was released for time served and got a job at the museum through a local program for offenders."

Jack shook his head. "Get an address. I'll arrange a raid while I'm in here. Stay in the camper. No need for these people to ask stupid questions."

I wondered what sort of call he needed to make. The communications in here are some of the most secure in the Bureau.

CHAPTER ELEVEN

"JACK CALM DOWN." The voice on the other end of the line was a bit annoyed.

"I am calm. What have you gotten me into this time? It was my understanding since the Demon Wars that the Thule Society was dead and gone. Why am I just hearing now from the victim of a theft no less, of a possible survivor? And one that might not age just like this woman?"

"Dietrich Eckart is confirmed as being inside the bunker when the Demon Prince was destroyed back in 1945. If he survived the aftermath of the war, this is the very first we are hearing of it. I promise you. We know that your memory is a bit spotty about Svartalfheim and the battle fought there, but those members of the Thule Group are gone for good. What have you learned about Miss Kelly?"

Jack glared at the ironically colored Red phone and put it back to his ear. "She's not a Witch or a Were. She was sitting in an outdoor chair made of steel, so that killed the Fae suggestion. She stood up in the daylight, so not a Vampire either. Daywalkers don't exist according to Anastasia, so she's not one of those. Agatha noticed that she looks to be in her forties now. Something funny about that. We are continuing to investigate."

"Good. Keep on it. What is your opinion of probationary Agent Blackmore?"

"She has good moves. They did a good job training her at Quantico. Did the local office send the report about what she found in the museum?"

"They did. According to their report, it was their own agents that stumbled upon it. I figured it was you. She has good instincts so trust her. Try and teach her what you know Jack. She and those like her are our future. Call if you run into problems. Good work so far." Jack heard a click on the other end of the line. Over twenty years he had run this one man division and the voice on the phone had only changed once. They were his lifeline, but he didn't like being kept in the dark. He hung up the phone and stepped out of the room.

"Agent Dalton, are you finished in there?"

"Yes. Thank you. You could have stayed, but it would have required you signing yet another secrets act document and possibly transferring to my department. I doubt you would enjoy it."

"Sounds boring. I'll keep this job thanks." The young technician opened the door to the secure communications room.

Jack passed through security and signed his badge back in.

"Hey Jack, thanks for the tip on the bodies at the museum!" Agent Jacob Phillips stood smiling next to the door.

"Did your team find other bodies?"

"Not your need-to-know there buddy boy! My bosses like it when I find cases we didn't know existed! Thanks for boosting my career. Have a good time chasing thieves."

Jack passed through the glass doors and started down the steps. "What an asshole." He realized he was starting to mutter to himself more than usual. It was almost time for another break.

"THAT IS CRAZY CHUCK! So she just let you process the entire scene?"

"She did. I finished with the room and kneeled down next to her by the body. Imagine my surprise when it stood up on its own and shook my hand. Just about scared the piss right out of me!"

"HA HA. Too funny! So it was all a joke then?"

"Sort of. It was a training exercise. Anastasia told me I was the first to get it right in years."

"Didn't you smell the other Vampire?"

"No. She's the only one I've ever met, and she has no scent. At least not to me. Cat said she smelled cold, but I didn't get any of that. This other guy was covered in a really strong cologne. All I could smell was pine trees. I swear one of my brothers wears the same thing."

"Do a good job for her Chuckles; she's one of my friends. I have to go. Catch you later." I could see Jack walking toward the RV. Hanging up the phone, I stuck it back into my spell bag.

The door rattled a moment, and Jack climbed back inside. "You ready to go?"

"Ready when you are. Did your phone call go well?"

"Not what I wanted to hear but yes. According to our records, Dietrich Eckart died in Berlin in 1945. If he's still around, this is the first that US intelligence has heard even a whisper of it."

"Then it's not him. I ran a deep scan on Bass."

"Anything pop up?"

"Just some mischief charges from his teenage years and one charge of attempted kidnapping."

"Attempted kidnapping? Was he charged?"

"Apparently not. I dug up the file. He's from a small town in backwoods North Carolina. He was arrested on a 10-14 and 10-15: Suspicious behavior and civil disturbance. The local police officers set up a sting involving a cop in a wedding dress. He had 'her' in the car and gone before he realized she was a he."

"That's hilarious! Why did they drop the charges?"

"The victim in all of this refused to press any charges. She was his ex. The judge gave him a choice: leave town or go to jail."

"So he left town and is now our problem."

"Yes. This is a bit out of character for him though. He usually just throws a rock at the window and runs."

"We have to check him out anyway; you know that. OK then. Back to the museum. By the way, the locals are pushing forward on their case against the Museum. Apparently, Jacob is in charge of it. He went out of his way to tell me they took all the credit."

I just shook my head. "That is just crazy. Aren't we all on the same team?"

He smiled at me. "My bosses are the ones that mentioned it. He may be taking credit, but they already knew it was you that broke that case regardless of what the 'official" report will say."

"It's still not right."

"No, it's not. You and those along with you are the new generation of Agents. Change it."

"I can try."

"You know what Yoda would say to that don't you?"

I hung my head. "Not you too? Just about every other thing out of my friend Chuck's mouth had something to do with those movies."

"It's a guy thing. You wouldn't understand."

"You got that right."

The museum parking lot contained a lot more government vehicles than last time. There was a forensics van setting up and everything.

"Looks like they are going all out for this case."

Jack glanced at the truck and other cars. "Not our case. They are here for the museum exhibit murders. It has the potential for headlines."

I just shook my head once again. We parked in the front this time a bit away from the maddening crowd of newsies and spectators. The rear exit was just as crowded. Local law enforcement barely said a word to us as we ducked under the yellow taped off entrance.

Several Agents were milling around the lobby as we walked straight through. We needed to find Bass and talk to him before any of the locals stumbled to him. I spotted the same Docent I talked to before.

"May I speak to you?"

"Whoa. Lady you just about got me fired! I'm not saying anything to you!"

"This has nothing to do with the exhibits. I just need to find one of the janitorial staff. An Ernest Bass. Have you seen him today?"

The Docent looked up at the ceiling for a moment. "Fine. That dude is a weird one, anyway. He hangs out down in Fashion and Housewares on lower level two. Most of us stay out of that area. Only art students hang out down there."

I motioned to Jack, and we headed for the stairs, less obvious that way. "He said we could find him down on lower level two."

According to the safety card on the wall, there were four lower levels to this place. Hopefully, we didn't have to chase Bass any; it looked like a maze.

"This Museum is a lot bigger on the inside. Ever watch Dr. Who?"

"Dr. Who, who? Is that a movie or something?"

"You like Star Wars but have never seen Dr. Who. What kind of man are you?"

"One that doesn't watch TV. In this job, I don't have much free time." We passed the doors for the first lower levels. There must be a really big freight elevator here somewhere because the door said Automotive History.

"You are missing a lot then. My roommate Cat gave me a crash course in science fiction in what little free time we had at the Academy."

"Is this the same Cat you keep telling me is a huge cat shifter?"

"She is."

"You will have to introduce me to her. She sounds like a resource for you."

"That and a really good friend. I think those are the doors we want." The double doors were propped open, and a long power cord stretched into the hallway. We followed the cord until we heard the music.

Singing an off-key version of 'Clementine' was a man in a jump-suit riding a floor cleaning machine. The machine was one of the old style ones with a wide round base and control handle. Ernest Bass was a small, extremely skinny, man that apparently didn't weigh very much. He was standing on the base of the machine holding on to the handle. The machine would swirl left or right, and he would be pulled along with it.

The cord we had been following had a knotted extension connection. I reached down and unplugged it. The machine lurched to a stop flinging Bass off to one side in mid-verse.

"Oh, My Darling..." This was followed by a loud thump! Our possible suspect hit the floor.

"Hey! What did ya go and do that for?" The little man picked himself up off the ground and approached us.

"Mr. Ernest Bass?"

"Howdy do to you and you. It's me, it's me, it's Ernest T.!"

"We are with the FBI. Can you answer some questions for us?"

"I can. What would you like to know?" He climbed up into one of the displays and sat down on the couch.

Smiling at his antics, I stepped up onto the stage. "There was a theft upstairs yesterday of a very expensive necklace belonging to Marilyn Kelly. Did you have anything to do with that?"

"Me? Why do you suspect me? I like the Goddess; she reminds me of Charlene."

"Who is Charlene?"

"My lost love. The woman of my dreams. She married someone else and not me!"

"We know you were arrested trying to break into Miss Kelly's house a few years ago. Why did you do that?"

"I just told you. Charlene, Charlene, how I miss you, Charlene. She ran off with a Dud!" He began to giggle uncontrollably.

"It looks like this might be a waste of time, Jack." I waited for Ernest to stop laughing.

"Ernest, do you know anything about the necklace and who might have taken it?"

He stopped laughing and looked me in the eye. "Anyone has it; it's Him." He waved his hands in a stopping or pushing motion. "I don't truck with Him. This is his place, not mine. I just clean things."

Jack stepped closer to the exhibit. "Who is Him? Is it one of the Managers?"

"Them? He laughs at them! Can't even see what is right in front of their damn eyes!" He started muttering to himself. I caught the word Haint and something about not crossing him.

"Ernest, what is it they can't see?" Jack peered at the little man.

"Ain't telling! Can't make me."

"I don't think Ernst is our culprit here."

Glancing at my boss, I agreed with him. "We could ask one of the managers. They might tell us what Ernest knows."

Jack made a face. "I didn't want to involve them since our brethren are dealing with them but I guess we need to while we are here. Let's get it over with." He walked to the elevator. Might as well be seen doing it.

THE ELEVATOR DINGED as it opened on the main floor. The noise and the opening doors caught the attention of several Agents as well as a couple members of the press. It seemed a small press conference was going on.

Agent Jacob Phillips took a nudge from his boss and intercepted us halfway to the administration entrance. "Hold up there Jack. You are intruding on our investigation."

"You don't even know where I'm going and you are trying to stop me. I'm not interested in your case other than to see justice done. I have my own to solve. But I do need to speak to someone in there." He pointed toward the door.

"Who do you need to speak to?" He looked at Jack suspiciously.

"What is it you said earlier? None of my business? Come along Agatha." He held the door open for me. Agent Phillips stopped it from closing and followed along behind us.

"I can zap him if you like."

"That would be pretty funny but no. He can follow if he likes." Jack paused at the door that said Human Resources.

He knocked and then opened the door carefully. "Hello? Is anyone here?"

A tall older Hispanic lady came out from around the corner of the office. "Oh, hello. What can I do for you today?"

Jack smiled at her. "Hello, I'm Special Agent Dalton and this in my partner Agent Blackmore. We would like to ask you a few questions about one of your janitorial staff."

"Of course Agents." She looked past us to Agent Phillips who tried to slip into the small room. "Can I help you, sir?"

The Agent jerked up in surprise and shook his head.

"Just ignore him, he's undercover." How Jack managed to say that with a straight face, I will never know.

She smiled at Jack. "What would you like to know?"

"We had a conversation with an Ernest Bass in the janitorial department."

The woman's face dropped. "Him. What has he done now?"

"Nothing like that. His name came up in the theft investigation in the Hall of Minerals. What is his story? He said a few strange things." We heard a door open and close, and I looked behind me. Agent Phillips was gone.

"Ernest came to us from one of the former Mayor's job programs. He was living on the street, and the program placed him with us. He has a few idiosyncrasies, but he does his job, unlike many other recipients of the yearly jobs programs. It if wasn't for some of them he would be a model employee around here."

"He mentioned someone called Him. When we tried to get him to explain, he muttered about not seeing and ghosts."

She shook her head. "He's a strange one. I don't even have to check his file about that one. He believes that a giant ghost or being lives in this museum. It's one of the reasons he only works on the lower floors. He will only come up here during business hours."

"That's interesting. Has anyone else mentioned seeing something like that?"

"We get crazies in here all the time, but the answer to that is no. Of course, I've only worked here for twenty years."

Thanking the woman we stepped out into the hall. "Where did Jacob go?"

"He stepped out when we mentioned Ernest. Do you think he'll try and arrest him?"

"Yes." Heading out to the main lobby, we reached it just as they dragged him out.

"Noooo. I didn't do it. It was HIM. He took it. I know he did! Look! Look! He's there." They had Ernest handcuffed and were dragging the little man out of the Museum.

Jack stepped in front of the group of Agents and yelled at them to stop.

"What are you doing?"

"This man has a history with Miss Kelly of breaking and entering. He even has old misdemeanor charges on his record. He had motive and opportunity."

"True. But you would not have even known about him if you hadn't been eavesdropping on MY investigation! We have already cleared Ernest here of any wrongdoing. This isn't even your case anymore Agent Phillips!"

The shouting match in the center of the main exhibit hall drew the attention of the local field office head and his press conference.

The newsies began yelling out questions to both Jack and the local Agents.

Ignoring all of them Jack leaned down and uncuffed Ernest. "You may go back to work Ernest."

"Hey! That is my prisoner. He is under arrest."

"No, he's not. I'm pulling rank on you. Magical Crimes has jurisdiction here."

Ernest rubbed his wrists and began hopping around pointing at the flying dinosaur exhibit. The big dragon dominated the display. "He's here. Here. Here. It wasn't me." He looked at us and ran for the stairs.

"Someone stop that idiot!" Two of the locals ran after him. I waved my hand, and they froze in their tracks.

"Do I need to arrest you for obstruction? I can do that, Jacob." Jack did not look happy. He looked at me and made a hand motion. I released the spell on the locals.

"What the bloomin hell is going on in here? Can't you see I have a press conference?"

"Sir, Agent Dalton here just let my prisoner go!"

"Which prisoner would that be Phillips?"

"The suspect in the Kelly necklace theft! The janitor. I told you about him; he had both a connection to the victim and opportunity. With his job at the museum he could have found a way around the security."

"Phillips, doesn't that case belong to Magical Crimes? We have our own murder investigation to conduct don't we?"

"But, Sir! You yourself told me to follow them and find a way back in. This guy is it. We wouldn't have even had the murder investigation if that Probi hadn't tried to arrest the manager first!" I smirked at the whole scene.

"I think that is quite enough, for now, Phillips! We can talk about this more at the office. Come along."

"But." The look on the local Director's face would have scorched paint. Realizing what he said on camera no less, Phillips blanched and followed after his boss. Half the newsies chased after them yelling questions.

I spotted the Manager I had grilled earlier and jogged over to him. Jack watched me go and turned to the reporters for a moment.

"Sir, can I have a moment. It's not about the murder investigation."

The haggard looking man sighed and nodded his head. "What do you need?"

"We are investigating the theft, and we spoke to Ernest, the janitor."

"That nut? He's a loony we can't fire because of the damned mayor. What did he say?"

"He mentioned someone who lives in the museum and no one knows is here?"

He chuckled. "He's been afraid of the upper floors since he started working here. Claimed he saw a dragon. He talks to it too. Or at least that is what the other janitors say. Foolishness if you ask me."

"Do you have a dragon display other than the one up there? Maybe that is what gave him the idea."

He gave me a funny look. Peering at my face, he replied. "Are you sure you are an FBI Agent? We don't have any dragon exhibits here in the museum. This is a place about Natural History, not mythology!"

"But what about?" I looked up and stopped talking. The dragon was gone!

The manager walked off in disgust. "Dragons indeed!"

"Did he tell you anything?"

Looking at Jack, I asked him. "What do you know about dragons?"

CHAPTER TWELVE

"Dragons?"

"The manager said that Ernest told everyone that a dragon lived in the museum. He said the other janitors say he speaks to it at night. When I mentioned the dragon display, I saw when we first arrived the manager asked me if I was a real FBI Agent. According to him, there is NO dragon display anywhere. This is a Natural History museum, not a mythological one."

"You saw a dragon in here?"

"I did. It was up there amongst the flying reptiles."

"Do you mind if we take this outside? There are far too many ears in here." I looked around at the milling reporters and local police.

"Sure." We pushed our way past the onlookers and slipped under the police tape. The RV was right where we left it except someone had draped crime scene tape around it and sealed the door.

"Idiots." Jack stormed toward the vehicle and was stopped by a local police officer.

"Sir, this is a crime scene."

"That, is my official vehicle. Why is it a crime scene?" Jack held up his Magical Crimes badge and identification.

"We were told by the local office that..." He looked at Jack's credentials. "We just got punked didn't we?"

"Most likely. They don't like us very much around here at the moment. Sorry."

The local police officer let us through and radioed his command about the situation.

We could see that someone tried to get inside the RV. There were pry marks all around both the main door and the truck doors. Even the windows looked scratched. Jack ripped off the sealing tape and tried his key. The door opened easily.

"I warded the RV."

"Nice. Can you do it all the time?"

"Sure. I normally do it for our dorm room and my lab on a regular basis. I don't want anyone messing with my supplies or Fergus."

We stepped inside. The refrigerator door was open, and Fergus was eating a head of lettuce.

"Fergus! Get out of there."

"Unicorn here. Did you forget it was feeding time? I get hungry!" I picked him and half eaten chunk of green leaves out of the cooler.

"How did you get in there?"

"I jumped." He looked pretty smug.

"Really? How did you open the door? It has a lock on it."

"I know stuff."

I shook my head. Unicorns. "Back in your barn. You can have hay; it is already in your stall."

"When can I have some real food? I miss my salad and pizza parties!"

"I might have a treat for you later."

He jumped up and down for a moment. "Hey, did you know a bunch of guys tried to break in here earlier?"

"What did they look like?"

"Do I look like an investigator? That's your job. It was just humans. I heard them grunting and cursing."

Jack came back into the dining area. "So you were mentioning dragons?"

"Dragons! There are dragons here?" Fergus ran into the barn and slammed the door with a Mooo.

I stared at the barn for a moment. "Yes. Dragons. As you can see from Fergus's reaction, they do exist. We don't know all that much about them even now. Grandmother told me they were very powerful and liked shiny, magical things. Her advice was to stay away from them. It is rumored in the magical community that one rules part of modern Russian. If one lives in the Museum, it would explain how the necklace went missing."

"That is all you know?"

"No. But I figured you wanted the basics. Every people and culture have their own version of dragons. The one I saw was a European or classic version. It has a total of six limbs; four legs and two wings. The head has horns and very sharp teeth. The classic dragons could speak. Ernest talks to it so it must have spoken to him at least once. They are omnivorous."

"Do you think it can change shape?"

"If it can it would explain how it gets in and out of here. It has to eat, unless it's using the cafe for everything." I tried to remember what I knew about dragons.

"Fergus get out here please?" There was no answer from the barn. I opened up the top and found Regina in the middle of the floor and no Fergus. I reached in and started moving things.

"Ouch!" I found him under the toy bed in the loft.

"Are you using Regina as bait?"

"Yes. The dragon can have her."

"I thought you loved her?"

He made a face at me and refused to answer that one.

"Come out here and talk to us. I promise we will protect you from the dragon." I removed my hand and closed the roof.

The door opened with a Mooo. "What do you want?"

"Dragons."

"Where!" The Unicorn tried searching the skies.

"Not here, calm down. What can you tell us about them?"

The mini-Unicorn settled down and scanned the ceiling of the RV. "They are the Unicorns natural enemies. They like to eat us and collect the horn. I love my horn, don't let it eat me."

"What else do you know?"

"They are smart. They talk like you and can look like humans. My great-great-great-great grandsire was once owned by a dragon. The story I heard was they use us as mounts then eat us! We have an instinctive fear of things that fly."

"That would make sense. Fergus, the spell that made you small also made you indestructible. You know this. It's why Zeus likes you so much."

The little guy glared at me at the name of grandmother's cat. He hated that animal with a passion.

"I can still be scared. They have Magick, lots of it. We can sense Magick. It's part of how we survive. Since I got small, my range isn't very far. I can sense something in that museum, but I can't tell you what it is. Am I done? I'm missing Pony Play!" He trotted back to his barn. Mooo!

"Why don't you take the sound maker out of that thing?"

"I've thought about it, but it's kind of funny."

"Did you know he could sense Magick?"

"That is new information, actually. I have had him for almost fourteen years, since I was seven. He was mad at me for a long time. We talk, but not about Unicorns. Maybe I should talk to him more often."

"Maybe you should. So how do we draw the dragon out?"

"I don't know." I stared off into space a moment. "Fergus?"

"I'm ignoring you." His voice was muffled, but still recognizable.

"Fergus. If dragons collect unicorns, that means they can sense you, right?"

The door slowly opened with a drawn out Mooooooo. "They can. We should go. He probably knows I'm here already." He looked around then trotted over to the window and peered at the museum.

I glanced at Jack and he was smiling. Nice to know we both had the same idea. "How would you like to help us catch a dragon?"

"No." He started back toward his barn. I grabbed him and stuck a kicking and thrashing Unicorn in my pocket. "This sucks!"

"Behave. We are going back inside. If you escape, it will be you all alone against the dragon. Do you want that?"

"No. Fine. Just don't let him eat me or keep me. OK?"

"Deal." Smiling at Jack, I sat back down.

"Can your Magick contain a dragon?"

"On the fly? No way. However, I could use my warding spell and freeze the entire museum. I would need to tweak it so we would stay free inside. Do you mind if I call my grandmother? I won't give her too many specifics."

"It's fine. Try and figure out something. If anything maybe we can make a deal with it to get the item back."

"Dealing with dragons is never a good idea Jack. Too many things could go wrong with that. Remember you are crunchy and taste good with ketchup to them." He laughed at my bumper sticker reference. Pulling out my phone, I started dialing Grams.

"Hello, Agatha."

"Grams, what do you know about dragons?"

"Straight to the point as always child. Dragons? Not very much. I remember teaching you to avoid them whenever possible."

"True. Except we think there is one living in a Museum in San Diego. We need to either capture it or talk to it."

"Interesting. I would strongly vote against capture. They are the living embodiment of at least two elements. They have magic beyond even me, child."

"That is what I told Jack, my boss. I thought maybe trapping it inside and forcing it to talk to us might work. Is it possible to be inside the ward while it's up and still have free movement?"

"Why would you... oh. I see what you intend to do. Very inventive dear. That might work. I suggest you test it first. But try envisioning a pocket inside the shell of your ward as you cast. Do not forget to leave air holes so you can breathe."

"Air holes? I wasn't aware it was non- porous. That could be an issue."

"Agatha, dear. Remember the fishing pails we used that one summer at the lake cabin?"

I paused at the non-sequitur. "Yes. What about them?"

"Remember how they allowed water in, but kept the minnows trapped?"

I remembered the yellow and white pails we had tied to the boat. We would lift the pail up, and water would stream out leaving enough for the fish to live in, but trapping them inside. I tried to envision my ward as a giant bait pail. I could see the air moving in-and-out of the holes. That might work.

"I think I understand. Thank you, Grams. Before I let you go, did you know that Unicorns could sense Magick?"

"It's good for you and Fergus to talk Agatha. He can teach you much. Good luck." I heard the click as she hung up the phone. She never answered my question. I stared at the little red barn for a moment more. How much did Fergus and grandmother talk?

"Jack, I think I have what may work. I need to test it. Would you like to be a guinea pig?"

WE DECIDED on his bedroom as the test bed for the spell. He would sit on his bed, and I would cast the spell around the room. With luck, he wouldn't be frozen to the bed. The standard version of this ward I was very familiar with. Only the changes might confuse me.

The first, second, third, and fourth versions of the ward were complete and utter failures. During each cast, Jack was frozen to the bed in mid-speech. I was starting to get the hang of it by version eight.

The previous two I managed to free first his eyes then his mouth. Version eight freed the whole person.

"That was very strange. I could see, feel, and hear, but everything was completely still. When I could move my eyes, it was the freakiest!"

"It was? Why?"

"A fly was frozen in mid-flight right in front of me. I could see its little eyes moving too."

That gave me a shiver just thinking about it. "What about when your mouth was free?"

"I couldn't breathe or talk. Just my mouth was moving. It felt like I was choking to death."

Making a mental note I tried to erase that variation. I didn't want to scare someone to death one day. "Do you mind if I practice number eight a few more times to lock it in?"

"Go ahead I can do paperwork." He pulled out his laptop and began typing.

I cast the spell ten more times to lock it into my brain. Each time I tried to trip myself up and varied the size and shape of the room. The last couple of times I set a time clock for the ward. I was worried about an accident that could trap me inside my own spell.

"Is it ready?"

"I think so. Want to go catch a dragon?"

"In the morning. It's too dark, and the museum has closed for the night." I looked out the windows at the darkness. Time flies when you are having fun.

"Do you want to move to that RV park we found or boondock here?"

"I think we'll boondock. Do we have enough water in the tanks?"

I checked the readout. "Looks about three-quarters full."

"OK. Run through the 'boondock checklist' and pull out the mini generator. I'm going to save the fuel in the truck; we might need to leave in a hurry." Boondocking is setting up an RV as lightly as possible in a parking lot, alley, or field. Usually, it was very primitive, with no exterior plumbing or electrical connections.

Grabbing the list by the door, I stepped outside. Checking off things as I went, I locked the wheels down and opened the generator compartment. The portable unit slid out of the compartment on a set of rails. I secured a special exhaust hose and checked the fuel levels. It started on the first try.

List completed I went back inside. Jack was still hard at work on his reports, but he had changed out of his suit. I slipped into my private bathroom and did the same. My workout outfit was good for sleeping in.

"Have you written up your reports yet?"

"Not yet." I stared out at the Museum.

"One of the best pieces of advice I can give is this. Get in the habit of doing your reports nightly. Many times when one case ends another begins. Better to get your thoughts down first while they are still fresh."

"That sounds like the voice of experience?"

"You bet. Trust me when I say doing multiple case files at the same time really sucks. Take a minute to think, then go work on today's events. Don't forget your personal diary either."

I thanked him and went to my bunk. His advice sounded good. I worked on the reports for as long as I could keep my eyes open. The typing came fairly easy.

As sleep claimed me, I thought this might be one for the record books. Capturing a live dragon.

It was the beeping and the sudden jerk that woke me up.

Beep, beep, beep, beep, beep. The RV shook and then the front lifted up. In my dreams, I was driving a garbage truck backwards.

"What the hell?" I rolled out of bed and looked down the hall toward the cockpit. A tow truck had just backed up and hooked us up. Grabbing my gun and credentials, I hit the door running.

"Stop! Federal Agent!" The tow truck driver froze in mid lift. Having a gun pointed at your head will do that.

"Why are you doing this? There are people in this thing."

Flipping my badge open, I waved it in his face. "Who told you to move this?"

"Lady, I work on consignment for the FBI. They tell me to move it; I move it. I got the order to move this from the local office this morning."

"Where are you supposed to take it?"

"My orders say the police impound yard."

"I'm telling you to forget your orders. This RV is still in operation."

"Let me see those orders, please." Jack was now alongside of me staring at the driver. They were quickly handed over. Jack glanced through them and handed it back.

The driver unhooked the RV and drove away. I watched him go and checked my ward thinking in the future I should increase the range.

"Do you know who did it to us?" Jack was making breakfast as I climbed back inside.

"Oh, yeah. The Director himself signed the order."

"Would you like revenge?"

"How? Tow their cars?"

"I was thinking a bit more devious. I noticed that they park in assigned spaces over there. How about I just move their cars for them?"

"Move them where?"

"I was thinking the roof of the FBI building. There is a helipad up there already, so the roof is reinforced for extra weight."

"How would they get them down?"

"Not my problem. A crane maybe?"

"I like it. It will have to wait until we bag a dragon first though."

"OK. I will hold you to that. My idea is we use Fergus as bait. He can ride in his usual spot and warn me if the dragon is near. I will tell you and close the ward. With luck, he will confront us to get Fergus or drop the ward. All we need is for him to expose himself." Jack chuckled at me.

"I meant for him to show up to other non-magical people. Pervert." His chuckle turned into a laugh at my comment.

It was super early still, and this place didn't open until ten. I set my alarm for eight-thirty and went back to sleep.

MORNING CAME MUCH EARLIER than I had anticipated. There was someone attempting to pound on our door. We experienced a brief moment of loud thumping noise followed by cries of protest. Agent Phillips was adhered to our door like a bug stuck on flypaper.

Looking out Jack laughed. He stepped outside. I watched as he explained to Jacob the predicament he was in. I waved my hand and dropped the extended shield I cast for the RV.

"You look like a bug on the windshield Jacob. What brings you out so early?"

"You can't park this thing here! It shouldn't even be here!"

"We intercepted your little minion by-the-way. Cute, towing the RV. It stays. What else you got?" The now confused man stumbled away from of our end of the parking lot.

"That was fun. Ready to catch Puff today?"

"I am, and so is Fergus." I patted my right breast. "I plan to reapply the ward when we leave just in case."

"Works for me. Let's go then." I grabbed my bag and raised the ward as I closed the door. Maybe we would catch another Agent?

CHAPTER THIRTEEN

THERE WERE ONLY a slight few patrons waiting for the doors to open. I watched each person carefully looking for signs of Magick. Fergus was awake and hadn't signaled me as of yet.

Several Agents were already inside when we came in through the front doors. "Why are you two back? We were told you finished your case."

"We haven't finished yet. The necklace is still missing. Who told you we were done?"

The Agent started to say, but stopped and shook his head. He glanced to his right and nodded. Looking around him, I could see our friend Agent Phillips. I touched the Agent's arm. "I understand."

Jack just shook his head at the exchange. I realized it could be difficult to be a regular Agent caught in the middle of a stupid political struggle. "Let's get this over with Agatha."

Nodding, I looked up toward the atrium windows. The flying dinos were there as was the large form of the Dragon. It really made me wonder how long he had been getting away with that little trick. According to the internet, the building had gone through several renovations and modifications since the Demon War.

The previous evening I had placed sigils all around the boundary of the museum. These were just small disks with a rune engraved upon them. I felt that they would help me to concentrate on such a large spell. In my mind, I brought each disk up and locked it into place. When all were there, I looked at Jack and nodded. Glancing upward, I said "læsa," activating the ward. I felt it close over the top of the museum.

A loud roar shook the walls and echoed inside the main hall. Visitors and Agents alike looked about in terror. A few yelled "earthquake" and ducked under exhibits. Jack stood fast beside me his hand gripping his sidearm. I looked up and could see the dragon start to move.

I felt a sharp pain in my chest and looked down to see Fergus stabbing at me with his horn. "The dragon is coming!" He ducked back down into my pocket.

"Did you hear that?" Jack nodded at me. I prepared some of my offensive spells but hoped I wouldn't have to use them. I wouldn't win against a creature made of Magick.

Another roar shook the building, and I looked up again. "He's starting to move."

"Dalton! What the hell is going on? What is causing that?" Agent Phillips got in Jack's face.

"That is the jewel thief. We just closed the door so he can't get out and now he knows it."

"The thief is making all that noise? What is it?" He was now looking all around the room.

"Agatha thinks it's a dragon. That's not the worst part."

"What's worse than a dragon?"

"Being locked in with one. He can't get out and neither can we."

There was a crashing noise above us. I looked up and could see the dragon thrash amongst the dino display. One of the pterodactyls came crashing down onto the gift shop kiosk.

"Everybody get under cover! Into the conference room!" Jack yelled at the other Agents to get the civilians under cover. It might not be an earthquake, but a pissed off dragon could do a lot of damage.

"Jack go ahead and help them! I will hide behind the Unicorn display."

"Unicorn? Where?" Fergus heard my yell and took that moment to poke out his head. He looked up and saw the stuffed Unicorn pawing at the air in defiance. "What sort of house of horrors is this?"

"That guy is long dead Fergus. I'm sorry I didn't tell you."

"Unicorns are people too! What right do they have to do that to one of my kind?"

"When this is all over I will let you give them a piece of your tiny little mind. OK?"

"Sure. That sounds good. Oh, there's a dragon here somewhere!" He ducked back into my pocket.

I LOOKED AROUND THE ROOM. An angry man was almost running toward me. He was wearing what appeared to be a 19th-century suit carrying a walking stick. I raised my hand, and a fireball appeared.

"That's far enough!" The man stopped in his tracks and laughed.

"You would threaten Me with fire? Really?" He took a couple more steps toward me.

I changed the ball to one of ice and cold.

His eyes widened. "Better. Interesting that you can do that. Most Witches cannot. What is your lineage?"

"I'm Agatha Blackmore Probationary Agent for the American FBI. You are under arrest."

"I asked your lineage, not your job, Agent Blackmore of the FBI." A fireball instantly appeared in his hand, and he threw it at me!

There were split seconds to act. For just a moment time seemed to stop as my brain changed gear and came up with a shield spell. I raised my arm to protect my face but was not in time. The fireball nearly touched my skin when a shield popped into existence on my arm. I had again forgotten the protector's bracelet! Sparks flew as it impacted and was absorbed.

"Where did you get that? Did Leomaris send you for me? You look like one of his."

I gave the dragon a funny look. "Who is that?"

"It doesn't matter if you don't know the name. Drop your ward and release me!" He tossed another fireball at me.

"Federal Agent! Drop your weapon and put your hands above your head!" It was at that moment that Agent Phillips decided to intervene.

"What fools you bring with you, Witch." He turned and breathed a gout of flame toward the local Agent. This time I was ready. I telekinetically tossed the Agent aside and launched my attack at the dragon.

Agent Phillips feet left the ground, and he flew toward the decorative fountain near the gift shop. I didn't pay attention to his landing which I am told was spectacular. My balls of ice caught the dragon by surprise. He roared his surprise. Readying my next spell I started yelling at him.

"If you stand down we can talk about this. You stole something that doesn't belong to you. We want it returned. Your living arrangements can be figured out with the museum. That is not why we are even here."

He laughed at me. "The trinket? All of this for a pretty bauble? Foolish child. It is not the trinket I want, but the spell it contains. My life is my own. Release the ward and I shall let you live."

"Sorry, but I can't. I took an oath." I tossed more freeze balls and readied one of the spells the Council gave me over the Winter.

"Your oath is meaningless if it is to these humans. Why do they matter so much to you?" He tossed a fireball at the humans hiding behind one of the dinosaurs.

I threw a shield spell that only covered the people not the display. The animatronic display continued to move, but all that could be seen were flames. There was a slight noise and water began to spray from above soaking my clothing. "Someone get these civilians out of here!" I yelled toward the back.

"They have abandoned you, Agent Blackmore. I am going to kill you and take that bracelet from you. It will make a fine addition to my collection." He said my name like it was something distasteful in his mouth.

Smoke and steam from his fires filled the air. It gave me an idea, but I would have to make up the spell. I could accidentally level the building if I wasn't careful. Fog I already knew how to make. I cast my spell on all the live planters and prayed to my Goddess.

Wisps of fog soon filled the room. I could barely make out the lights from outside and the various exit signs.

"Why make it harder to see? I can kill you in the dark if I have to. Don't you know that Dragons never give up their hoard to anyone?"

"What horde is that? All I see is a bunch of old bones and modern appliances. Someone told me that your people rode Unicorns into battle and treasured the horns. Dragons are supposed to have rooms of gold and treasure hidden away. Where are those? Why steal from the museum?" I ducked under one of the displays.

"Silly girl. This place is my horde. Who do you think provided the money to build it? Where did the things in it come from? I have been here the whole time. I even watched as they used MY home to treat broken humans during the war. This is my home! If it is in my home, it belongs to me! Why do you think I wanted it back?" Another gout of flame flared to my left. The fog was getting thicker and harder to see through.

I prayed to the Gods to grant me strength and make my aim true. "Artemis and Demeter guide my aim and grant me the power of the element of Earth!" I tossed a handful of salt and herbs into the air and directed my will toward the dragon.

"What are doing little Witch! I can feel you." He sent a series of fireballs straight at me just as my spell took hold. He began to scream, and gigantic wings shot out of his back! Twisting and almost writhing in pain he began to shift into his dragon form.

"What have you done? NOooo!" His gurgling scream shook the building as my spell finally took hold. I had to cover my ears to block out the sound. There was a loud crackling sound and then silence. I crawled out from under the display of ironically, serpents, and stood up. I took several deep breaths and centered myself.

That last spell used up all my energy and that of Fergus as well. He was in his pouch sleeping it off. Our fight had taken us toward the rear of the Museum. Where there had once been beautiful stained glass was now a wall of black granite blocking out the light. Faint shapes could be seen on its surface. The glass was completely transmuted to stone. Stone table and chairs were scattered about. Even the carpet was stone. Standing in front of the wall was what looked like something from a horror movie. A giant stone dragon caught in mid shift, his body twisted and grotesque. Giant stone wings thrust from the half-human-half-lizard body. I staggered a moment and sat down on one of the former couches now stone benches. It was there that Jack found me.

"Agatha, are you alright?" I was still staring at the dragon statue I created.

"I'm OK. Just tired."

"What happened to the dragon?" I pointed to the statue. Jack just stared.

Fog still clung to the floor giving the entire museum a ghostly look. The fires were all out, and the smoke had cleared. I could hear sirens and people noise coming from outside.

"Is he dead?" Jack moved closer and was peering at the former man.

"I'm not sure? When Fergus wakes up, we can ask him if he senses anything."

"What happened to the window and the furniture?"

"Accidental discharge. It happens. The magic caught him full on, but there was collateral damage." The wall was actually very pretty with the shapes and swirls from the stained glass.

"Jack, did you hear what he said about the museum?"

"Sort of. He was pretty loud."

"He said the money to build it came from him. He lived here somewhere. We may still be able to find the necklace."

"We will have to search. Could he hide something and not have others see it?"

"He had more power than me, of course, he could have. I think the upper floors hold our answer." I looked closer at Jack. His suit coat was gone. Soot and smoke marks covered his shirt. "Did the civilians all get out?"

"Not yet. Can you drop your ward? The fire department needs to get inside."

"Oops. Sorry, I forgot." I made a hand motion and said a word of power.

Outside the firefighters pushing against the ward suddenly fell inward. They rushed the building along with police and rescue workers. Panicked tourists and staff ran the opposite way trying to escape. Basically mad chaos.

A dripping and wet Agent Phillips came over to stare at the dragon. "What the hell is this thing?"

I sleepily stared at the soaked Agent and smiled. "That is our thief. A real honest to Gods Dragon."

"There is no such thing as dragons!"

"Well since one just about turned you into a charcoal briquette, you would, of course, know better than I." I tried not to be sarcastic.

"Jacob go away! My case not yours." Jack glared at the man.

We all turned our heads toward the middle of the room as firefighters ran in with hoses and began soaking down the planters. Fog continued to billow out regardless of how much water they sprayed.

"Uh, Jack?"

"Yeah?"

"Could you tell them that isn't smoke and water won't put it out?"

He laughed as one of the heavily dressed crew lifted a plant out of the display and stared at it. Wisps of fog still poured from nothing as he held it. "Never mind. I think they figured it out."

I watched as one of the local Agents pointed in our direction and several rather mad firefighters stormed toward us.

"What the hell is going on in here?" They thrust the smoking plant at us.

"There was a very pissed off dragon, and he was shooting flame everywhere. I cast a fog spell to distract him and give me some cover. The fires he caused are out. I think the sprinklers took care of that. The fog? Well, the last time I cast that spell it took a full day to stop, sort of. Water won't put it out. Sorry."

The one man and one woman in bunker gear just stared at me. They looked at Jack with a pleading look.

"She's really an FBI Agent, and she is telling you the truth. The dragon is over there." He pointed at the statue.

They both just stared at the statue and at us. Muttering about insane people they walked back to the rest of the firefighters. The others were loading a cart with the smoking pots and took them outside. The real fires could now be seen. They used axes and water to finish those off. Agent Phillips had wandered off somewhere, and Jack sat down next to me.

"During the fight, he said there is a spell on that necklace. He said he wanted it more that the necklace. He asked if someone sent me after him."

Jack perked up. "Did he say who?"

"Leomaris. Does it mean anything to you?"

"No. Not at all. I'll add it to the report when I write it up. Feel like looking for his lair?"

"Can I rest for a minute more?" I looked down at my clothes. They were scorched and torn. I slipped my jacket off and tossed it aside. Like Jack's my white shirt was scorched and smoke stained.

"This job is sure hard on the clothes. Let's go look before your friend Jacob comes back." I stood up and followed him toward the elevators. They were still on so we went all the way up to the top first.

The top floor was devoted to textiles and woven things. I could see the hanging wires that once held the flying dino replicas. I tried to judge the length of the room. "Jack? How long is this room supposed to be?"

A door was hidden under a thirteenth-century tapestry of St George fighting a dragon. It was flush with the wall and looked to be part of the original construction. It opened to a display hall that would make any curator below green with envy. Artifacts from all ages lined the walls and sat in boxes on the floor. He must have collected for years to amass this much. It would take days or weeks to find the necklace in all of this. But at least we knew it was here. Jack had me seal the room.

We would tell the museum's directors when the smoke settled. We took the elevator down and got off on the main floor.

"There they are!" Heads turned as we stepped off the elevator.

"I demand you be arrested for trying to burn down the museum!" Agent Phillips grabbed Jack's arm.

Jack looked at the smug looking Agent and shook his head. "Did you not watch any of the surveillance videos or see the dragon that turned into a man then back to a dragon? He got changed mid shift stone back there." Jack pointed.

Even more heads turned toward the statue. "If you lay another hand on me I'm going to break it!" Jack pried the man's hand off him.

I stepped around him and Jack. The Agent reached out another hand and grabbed MY arm. He fell over with a loud clank. "No one touches the Witch."

"Did you just?"

"He'll be fine in an hour or so. I used a different spell on him."

"Now see here, you can't walk all over my Agents like this and get away with it! I demand you face charges for all this destruction!" The local Director was backed up by his usual news-crew.

Jack whipped out his phone and called a number. He handed it to the Director. "Here, it's for you."

133

The man took the phone and held it to his ear. "Hello?" The phone stopped ringing, and a voice started to ask him questions.

"Yes, Sir! No. No. No, Sir! Yes, I understand. Yes. I apologize for my Agents. No. Sorry. Yes. I do. I understand." He hung up the phone.

Handing the phone back, the Director said he was sorry. The news crews waited for him to make a statement, but he pushed them away and had them removed from the scene.

At my look, Jack smiled. "It pays to have connections."

CHAPTER FOURTEEN

"WHAT THE HELL are we supposed to tell the public?" The head of the Board of Directors at the museum, along with local law enforcement stood staring at the new statue at the rear of the museum. He turned to stare at Jack and me. "The contents of this dragon's hoard are beyond anything this museum has ever had to deal with. Our curators are still recovering from the shock of what was right beneath their noses for so long. What do we do?"

The arguments had actually been going on for several days. Once everyone watched the security camera footage and saw the new stone window, the arguments and repercussions began. This was just the latest of the meetings. I was growing tired of the whole thing and really wanted to move on.

The local FBI Director was jumping at the bit to get in front of cameras again and take the glory for his department whether it was deserved or not. "I say we just tell them the truth and let it go. This is California; strange things happen all the time."

"And you think that will work? Just like that? It was a Dragon that caused it. He lived here!" This was from the head investigator appointed by the Mayor of the city.

"We have to say something?"

"No, you do not. You will say nothing." All the heads in the room turned toward the new voice that literally appeared in the room. Standing next to the statue was a tall man in a vermilion robes. He carried himself with great importance and spoke with a slight British accent. I recognized his tone. When I had last seen this man, he was storming away from me declaring me a menace. His name was Montgomery.

"Who the hell are you?" The Director of the FBI stood and started to approach Montgomery.

He waved his hand, and the Director froze. I could see his eyes moving so he was still conscious. "I shall be taking all of this with me. You are not to be trusted with any of this; you will only harm yourselves."

"Gentlemen, this is Montgomery, he represents the American Witches Council." I figured I should step in before trouble started.

He glared in my direction. "The name is Magnus Montgomery Windsor to be clear. I represent the Council in all things in relation to this mess."

"What right do you have..." With a wave, time seemed to stop for everyone in the room except me.

"Why did you do that?"

Surprised Montgomery looked back at me. "Inconceivable. You are not powerful enough to withstand that spell." He peered at me with now beady eyes.

"Why freeze them? They just wanted to know who you were."

Walking across the room, the Magus circled me as he talked. "I told the rest that you were trouble. This experiment of theirs should never have been conceived. You are a menace and should be locked away. But no, I was overruled by those that should know better. Now you have done it. You have all but declared war against the Draconic Empire. No one can see what the repercussions of this will be!" He pointed at the statue.

"Did you know?"

"Know what?" He thundered at me.

"That there was a dragon living here. Did the Council know?"

"Of course we knew you insolent child. We have known for over a century of his presence in this city. Now is the time for damage control. Those he reports to may or may not notice his absence. We have days or years before they act. And once again it is all your fault!" The Magus spoke a word and pointed at me. A ball of flame flew at me faster than anything I have ever let go myself. I could only raise my arm and try to deflect it.

There was a bright, blinding flash like a thousand flashbulbs going off at once. I was temporarily blinded, all I could see was a giant white dot. Blinking my eyes, I could sort of see if I squinted. Magus Montgomery was staring at me in shock. Covering me was a shield projection. The protector's bracelet glowed on my wrist like a beacon. I slowly lowered my arm. The shield flickered for a moment and disappeared.

"Where did you get that?" Montgomery pointed at my arm. "That is Council property young lady! You will give it back right now!"

I stared at one of the old men that haunted my nightmares. Remembering what grandmother told me, I shook my head. "No, the bracelet is mine. It belongs to the Blackmore clan and cannot be removed. Take what you came for and go." I readied myself for battle knowing that if it came to blows, this man would grind me to dust, bracelet or no bracelet.

Montgomery glared at me as he cast his transportation spell. "We will speak of your disrespectful nature another time Miss Blackmore. Bet on it." He raised his hands and vanished in a flash of smoke and light. The dragon vanished with him. I didn't run to check, but I'm sure the hoard went as well.

"What just happened? Where did the dragon go? Who was that guy?" Those were some of the more polite questions when the room woke up from the spell that froze them. I explained who he was, leaving out his attack on me personally. I wasn't believed until the security tape was played. I guess my word is not my bond yet.

"I wondered if the Council would show themselves."

"Why do you say that Jack?"

"Too much Magick was involved here. Regardless of what this Montgomery said, I think the dragon's appearance was a shock to them. They might have warned us off if they really knew he was here. Do you think they will retaliate against you?"

"The Council? I doubt it. They are scared of Grandmother for some reason. I'm more worried about this Draconic Empire Montgomery mentioned. That name implies there are more dragons around."

"Didn't you say though that this one was worried you represented someone?"

"Yes. Leomaris. I checked our databases and came up with nothing."

"Hmm. I'll run it past Washington along with the name Draconic Empire. They may know something that isn't in the files. It wouldn't be the first time." Jack frowned and stared at the floor. "You should have mentioned that the Council Representative tried to kill you."

"It wasn't the proper time. I really wanted to limit questions about my bracelet. It's bad enough the Council knows about it now." I ran my hand over the object in question. I would almost swear it purred like a cat for just a moment.

"I will try and keep it out of my reports. You realize it saved your life? Regardless of the Council's orders or opinion, that man dislikes you enough to kill you. What did you do to piss him off that much?"

"I really have no idea. I followed his instructions to the letter when he was my instructor a few years ago. In casting the spell, some animals were fused into a new creature. He refused to accept any blame, and I never saw him again until now. I was as surprised as you to see him here."

Looking around Jack stared at the local politicians and legal representatives for a moment. "Let's get moving, shall we? We still have to give Miss Kelly the bad news."

"She isn't going to be happy with us."

"No, but she can get in line. These folks will most likely blame us too." He swirled his finger around.

I nodded. A sharp kick and poke to my breast reminded me of something. "Jack, do you mind if I stop by the curator's office? Fergus wishes to say something to them about Unicorns."

Jack chuckled. "That should freak them out. I'll be out in the parking lot. Don't take too long." He headed out toward the outer doors. I went through the ones that said 'Staff.'

Knocking gently I stuck my head in the head curator's office. "Curator McPhee?"

"Yes, may I help you?" The voice came from behind a large desk in the middle of the office. Preserved animal parts in jars and boxes lined the walls of the office. A large picture of the curator dressed in safari gear dominated the room. I stepped into the room.

"Sir, I'm Agent Blackmore with the FBI. An associate of mine wishes to speak to you about the Unicorn exhibit."

"Really?" The curator was a man of medium build wearing an impeccably tailored suit. He sat up and straightened his jacket. "We are very proud of our exhibit. I was part of the team that acquired the animals. I am very troubled by the fire damage, but we have others we can replace it with for now."

"Yes, Sir. It was that part of the exhibit that he wished to speak to you about."

"Well, where is this person?"

"Right here." I reached into my pocket and pulled out Fergus. He allowed me to set him on the desk before he lit into the man.

"What the hell gives you the right to capture and kill my people? Is it the fact that we don't talk and communicate like you humans?" The mini Unicorn stormed across the desk and was pacing back and forth as he talked.

"Agent Blackmore. what is this?" The man peered at Fergus like there were strings attached.

"This is Fergus. He is sort of my familiar. I accidentally shrank him when I was seven."

"Ignore her! This is between you and me. Well? What do you have to say for yourself? Wish to apologize? There are so few of us to begin with, and now you have to kill us too! What gives you the right?"

Still ignoring Fergus he stared at me. "He is a real Unicorn?"

"He is! And I'm down here you bozo! Stop pretending I don't exist and talk to me not her!" The curator looked down at him and reached out a finger as if to poke him.

"Sir! I wouldn't do... that." It was too late. Fergus turned and charged the man stabbing him in the finger with his horn.

"Ouch! Damn it!" Blood spurted across the desk as he shook his hand in surprise.

"Score one for our team! No one pokes the Unicorn!" Fergus danced away from him shaking his head and horn like a pissed off bull during a fight.

"Sir, I'm sorry about that." I scooped up my charge and placed his protesting ass back in my pocket. "He just wished to give you his opinion. I need to go. Cases to solve and all that. Thank you for your time." I backed out of the office as the man struggled to apply a band-aid to his finger. Muttering to himself the entire time.

Jack had the motor running and was parked in the unloading zone in front of the museum. "Did Fergus talk to someone?" Putting the RV in gear, he began to pull out of the parking lot.

"He did. He got to attack and draw blood too. The man was too concerned over whether Fergus was real than what he could tell him about Unicorns."

"I can see that." Jack could see several of the bone-pickers exiting the museum and start to chase the RV. "I guess they didn't realize the resource he could be."

"That is what I thought. Their loss. Don't forget to swing past the FBI headquarters here."

Several of the out-of-shape museum staff had dropped out of the chase and lay panting in the parking lot. Jack smiled as he turned out onto the expressway leaving the last of the sprinters behind. "Why did we need to go there?"

I smiled. "That project we talked about? We talked about a nice thank you for not towing our vehicle? Do you remember?"

"Oh, yeah. That. We should wait until after lunch. Let's get the visit to the starlet out of the way first."

"OK. You're the boss."

The rest of the trip back out to Miss Kelly's house was uneventful. I could see how traveling from location to location could be addictive. The scenery kept changing.

The familiar gates loomed in front of us. Jack mentioned our names to the box on the gate and they swung open. "Less of a hindrance this time. I hope she isn't too mad at us."

"She could apply to the Council for its return. It is a stolen item after all. They might give it to her."

"That is true. They might." He parked in front of the house like last time. Max was once again waiting for us.

"Agents. Madame is awaiting you in the salon. Please follow me." He led us through a different part of the house to a small room overlooking the ocean. Miss Kelly was lying on a covered day bed. We could see a darkened shape, but that was all.

"Miss Kelly?"

"Welcome back Agents. Did you find my necklace?" Her voice was cracked and broken she sounded hoarse.

"Sort of. The thief was a dragon that lived inside the museum."

"Really? I find that rather fantastical. Are you sure?" Her voice sounded worse than before.

"Yes. Ma'am. I fought him myself. He had a lair built into the very walls of the museum. They had no idea he was even there."

"Did you find my necklace?"

"We had begun to search his belongings when all of them were seized by the American Witches Council. One of their Agents appeared and took the lot with him. I am very sorry ma'am. We can't give you your property back. Agatha had a suggestion that you could apply to them for its return. You are the victim of a theft after all. They may give it back to you. Besides, you have a personal connection to a member. Remember?"

There was a moment of silence. "I may do just that if I have the time. I'm afraid they may refuse me when they examine the item."

"Ma'am, the dragon said something to me about it. He said he only wanted the spell it contained not the necklace itself."

"Secrets are so hard to keep. That spell cannot be removed. Did he say what the spell was Agent?"

"He didn't. Just that he needed it. What was it?"

"Let me show you so you understand." She sat forward and pulled back the cover. Instead of a young, never aging Goddess of film, sat an old woman. "Over five-hundred years ago a Spanish explorer and ship's Captain searched for the fountain of youth. He never found it or maybe he did. The necklace appeared in Spain after his death in the possession of his family. Unlike many of the treasures from Central America, it wasn't broken up. The jewels and especially the amulet were kept whole as a family heirloom. It passed through many hands over the years; none realized its true power until it literally fell into mine. I will not tell you when. That will stay my secret. I didn't need to wear it, just keep it near and in my possession. That was one of the requirements. I think you can guess the rest."

Everything clicked in my brain as she told the story. I began to nod. It made sense to me why the dragon wanted it. Who didn't want to live forever? "It allowed you to stay young."

"It did. I allowed my vanity to get the better of me in the 1970s. I almost quit acting during that time period. They wanted older more mature looking actresses for all the real movies. Teeny-bopper movies are always popular, but not the dramatic roles. Not like the ones in the previous decades. I should have trusted what my advisers told me and gave up acting. I allowed the necklace out of my possession for a few days to age my body. It worked, and the roles became mine. The recent exhibit was for the same reason. It was to be my last hurrah. The best movie script I ever read. I wanted it so badly I allowed myself to age. Now look at me. Karma is a real bitch."

"Miss Kelly we are sorry..."

"Forget it. I'm just a bitter old woman who, if my doctor is to be believed, has very little time left to live. Leave me to enjoy what I have left. Just go." She waved us away.

The ever present Max stood by the door. "Agents, I will see you out."

"Max what will happen to you?" The man flinched and turned toward me.

"Whatever madame wishes. My family has served her since before what you call the Demon War. She found us in one of the dictator's camps and rescued us. She is everything to us. Goodbye Agents." He closed the door behind him as we walked out to the RV.

Looking back as we pulled away I thought I saw her standing out on the balcony. "I guess that solves your mystery for you, Jack."

"It does. My bosses won't be happy either. I'm sure they would have wanted it for themselves. I wonder what else the dragon had hidden away up there?"

"Nothing that should have been let loose in the world I'm sure. The Council may have had a point. I guess we won't ever know will we?"

"Nope."

"So do we have a new case yet?" I wondered where we were going next.

"We don't yet. I'm going to backtrack just a bit and head toward Texas. I haven't seen my wife in several months and would like to. Dallas is about twenty hours away. I'm not going to drive straight through this time. We are. You get to use that driver's license for once."

"I do? Cool."

"If you call driving ten hours straight fun then OK. We will make a few stops along the way. Now I have the first leg of the drive. You get the second ten hours or so until we get just outside Dallas. Traffic around that area is a nightmare, so I will take over for you then. Plus I can drive straight to where my wife lives. You might want to rest up a bit."

I crawled into my bunk and watched the scenery roll by out the window. Another case over and done with. I would take a short nap then tackle the reports.

"She is in possession of what?"

"There is a Guardian bracelet on her arm." Montgomery stood in front of several Council members. They were gathered inside a vast library filled with the knowledge of the ages.

"How did you discover this?" The speaker was an older woman with silver hair. She scowled at Montgomery. "Damn it! You attacked her, didn't you? In defiance of our orders?"

"She is a child! We should have locked her powers down, not encouraged her! We have done as much in the past. I was justified. She defied me."

"Those were remarkable circumstances and you know it. Besides, she is a Blackmore. I'd like to see you try to slip that past Marcella Blackmore; she would gut you like a pig."

"I'm not afraid of that woman!"

"You should be, I am. Regardless. Did you get all the items in their possession?"

"I did. They had yet to classify much of it. Magical diagnostic of the dragon is inconclusive. He may still live."

"That is unfortunate. I had hoped we might recover him. I cannot believe we missed his presence! How many more did we miss? Did the girl know anything?"

Montgomery didn't look at the other Council members he looked up at the ceiling. The murals that decorated it were nice, but not that nice.

"You didn't ask her did you?"

"She is just as arrogant as she was two years ago! She doesn't respect her betters."

"Montgomery forgets that I read the report that Marcella submitted about the creatures that were changed. She included the spell that he himself wrote. The words were incorrect as the girl said."

"That is a damned lie! I do not make those kinds of mistakes! Damn you Fitzgerald."

The cocky looking Frenchman smiled as Montgomery squirmed in front of the others. They had been at odds for years.

"Stop you two! You both forget the issue at hand. What does the girl know that we do not? And is the Draconic Empire a threat?"

"It has always been a threat, Ray. We just were unaware that there was a dragon there. We need to dig into the records and find him. His possessions may lead us to more. Send a message to Marcella. She can control her granddaughter, let her ask the questions we want to know."

"Fitz, she may not help us this time."

"If Leomaris and the Draconic Empire attacks us it is their problem as well as ours."

"When has the Greater Council ever cared about that? They only care about species, not politics." Ray Winters shook her head. This entire conversation was like playing with fire.

"We can only try. You have known her the longest."

She snorted. "Like that matters. I will try. You better hope they don't attack. The mundies are the least prepared of all of us."

Barry Hutchison was the vice director of the San Diego branch of the FBI. He was actually having a good day. His boss was in big trouble with the local museum board and all of his illicit TV contacts. The fight at the museum made him look very bad in front of his superiors and the newsies. Whenever Magical Crimes gets involved, bad things always happen. It was all he could do not to shake his head. Even Washington was mad at him. Barry was excited that he might have a new job soon. Throwing his boss under the moving bus was the right thing to do. He was in such a good mood that he skipped lunch and decided to go home early today.

"Where's my car?" The space it usually occupied was empty. In fact so were all the assigned spaces. He pulled out his clicker and pressed the button. He heard his car make the iconic wolf whistle he had specially installed, but could not see it. Pressing the button numerous times he almost broke his toe kicking a trash receptacle. Where was his car? Yanking out his cell phone, he made a call.

"Security office. How may I help you, Sir or Ma'am?"

"This is Assistant Director Hutchison my car appears to be stolen."

"Sir. Where was it located when you noticed it missing?" The security officer sat up straighter in his seat and pulled out a report tablet.

"It was in the parking lot in my assigned space! Why else would I call you?"

"Excuse me, Sir? Did you say it was taken from our lot?"

"Of course I did you idiot! Get someone out here now!" The assistant director closed the phone thinking about the sort of people that worked for the security department. Maybe it was time to clean house in there.

With a screech of tires, a security golf cart tore into the parking lot and stopped at the front lot. A slightly overweight officer got out. "Director Hutchinson?"

"Over here. My car was right there!" He pointed to the empty space next to an entire line of empty spaces.

"Have you asked any of the other owners if they saw anything?"

"Isn't that your job? It's what we pay you for."

"Yes, sir." The security officer poked and prodded the trash cans.

Barry just shook his head. Did he expect to find it in there? He pulled his phone out again.

"Director, sorry to bother you, but my car seems to have been stolen. I wondered if you saw anything?"

"Why ask me that? How could I see anything?"

"Well yours is gone as well, and I assumed you left with it."

"What?"

The conversation devolved from that. Local police were called as well as the entire investigative branch of the local FBI, many of which were the victims.

"Sir, can you tell us where you and the other Agents were during the theft?" The local police Captain took the case himself. He was the only one who could keep a straight face. The FBI Agents were not very popular around here.

"We were working."

"Yes, Sir. Now did I overhear correctly that your clicker works for your car?"

"It did, I think the battery ran down. I had the lot searched before you appeared. It is not here at all. I don't understand how we could hear it."

"Yes, Sir. I have requested a chopper. Maybe they can spot it."

"Good. It has to be here somewhere."

The San Diego police department was lucky. A local company had gone bankrupt and donated two brand new helicopters to the department as a tax write off. Pilots had been trained, and the choppers painted. They were the envy of many smaller departments in the area.

"Are you seeing what I am?" The co-pilot was new.

"If you mean about a dozen cars parked on the roof of the FBI building then yes. I see it too." He pulled out a cell phone and quickly snapped a picture. He sent it first to the Captain but spread it around the department as it was too classic not to share.

The Captain sat in his patrol car laughing his ass off. Whoever did this should get a medal. He hoped they were far from here because these were Government Agents and they were going to be pissed.

"Excuse me, Director?" The Agents looked like a glee club out in the parking lot. In their almost identical suits, they all turned to look at him.

"Yes? Did you find them?"

"We did. They were here all the time. Since this is on your turf, we will leave you to it. My men will take down the tape." He turned to leave and waited for the protests.

"Now see here! You say they are here? Where?"

The Captain pulled out his phone and showed them the picture. All twelve cars were lined up on the roofs of the cars spelling out the word 'tow.' "Did you piss off a Witch or something?"

The Director just stared at his building and screamed.

CHAPTER FIFTEEN

THE PARKING GARAGE was darker than usual. Benjamin Raines made a mental note to send a note to the maintenance staff. There was a faint clicking noise echoing as he took each step. He stopped and checked the bottom of his shoes for tacks. Shaking his head as he set each foot down he thought to himself he was getting paranoid in his old age. It was this new deal his company was negotiating. Business was business. That is all that mattered. 'Make money' is what his dearly departed father would say to him if he was still around. What they were doing was not illegal. It wasn't even immoral. It made good business sense. He looked around the garage. Why the executive parking was so far back still surprised him. He was the president of the company, he should be able to park where he wanted, fire regulations be damned! His Jaguar was the first in line. Hitting the clicker his car started up, and the doors opened on their own. Of all the American ingenuity available; that was one of his favorites. Glass tinkled behind him, and he turned.

"Hello? Is anyone there?" There was nothing but silence. "Must be a cat or something." He muttered to himself. He turned back toward the car and screamed.

The only sound in the garage was his car's running motor. He lay on the floor of the garage gasping out his last breath as his blood dripped from his body. No one was there to hear him. That was how security found him during their hourly sweep.

I WAS asleep and having a nice dream. It was the harvest parade back in Blackbriar Heights. I was riding in one of the horse-drawn carriages. I could hear the clip-clop noise of the hooves on the street and feel the bumpy road on the carriage wheels. It was the sharp pain in my side I didn't understand. I opened my eyes.

The shades were open, and I could see out the window into the street. I would almost swear I drew those before falling asleep. Fergus stood on the window sill trotting back and forth. He jabbed me with his horn.

"Hey! Stop that!" I rubbed my side and realized it was sore in multiple places.

"It's about damn time you woke up! Time to feed the Unicorn! Not sure about you since you don't seem to eat but I like food!"

"I eat. What time is it?"

"Do I look like I'm wearing a watch? It's feeding time for the Unicorn. That is all I care about."

I swung my legs out of the bunk and moaned. They were not the most comfortable of beds. Staring at my cell phone, I noticed it had been way longer than ten hours. I ignored Fergus and walked up to the RV's cockpit area.

"Jack? You forgot to wake me up."

"I didn't forget. Washington called, we have a very urgent case in Las Vegas to get to. I figured you would want to be sharp for the investigation." I sat down and buckled myself in.

"You need to sleep too, Jack. What is the case about?"

"Straight to the point. Good girl. It has all the hallmarks of either murder or an assassination. I'm leaning toward the latter." He had his eyes on the road and barely looked in my direction.

"A murder? What happened?"

"A very important oil executive was killed in his own company's parking garage. It has all the hallmarks of a Were kill. The trouble is that garage is one of the hardest places to get inside of. It was not an accident that a Rogue was inside. This was either a hunt or a contract kill. It falls under our purview."

"So we have to hunt a Were down?" All I could think about was what both Cat and Chuck had taught me about Weres.

"Yes, we ultimately do. Is that going to be a problem for you?" He slowed the RV down and glanced at me.

"No. If they have broken the law, they should be punished. Even Pack Law is against killing mundanes, much less for money."

"Good. I will need you to scan for clues and to help track. If this is a contract kill, there won't be very many of those."

"Does this happen a lot?"

"Contract kills or assassination?" At my nod, he sighed. "Some. Usually, it is one pack versus another. We capture the rogue and the pack Alphas face censure from the government or other packs. It's usually kept quiet and internal. Gotta love the intricacies of Pack politics."

"What about assassinations?"

"That is something else entirely. Normally the regular FBI handles those. But because the killer is a Were we take it. They are going to fight us worse than usual for this one. Much worse."

"Why? I would think they would want to hand it off to us."

"Politics again. The human kind. The company is Tri-States Developments they are the ones behind the Lockpoint oil pipeline."

"Is that the one in the news that people are losing their minds over?"

"It is. I'm not sure what this man's death will do to the negotiations, but it won't be pretty."

I grimaced. "Wonderful. Do you mind if I check with Cat? She might be able to clue me into Pack politics and dealing with Rogues and assassins."

"You may. Keep the usual OPSEC, please." I told him I would. I waited until he stopped at a red light before getting up and moving. Safety first.

"Aggy what the hell have you gotten involved in now?" Cat was on her internship just as I was. Hers was of a more investigative nature. She up in St Louis helping track down a serial killer.

"Jack, my boss out here said it's just Pack politics."

"Yeah, dirty politics. My uncle never got involved in anything like that to my knowledge. But dad told me about it."

"Any idea what I'm about to go after?"

"Maybe? There are European Packs that specialize in that sort of training. They are for hire to the highest bidder. It's a heritage sort of thing. Very much frowned upon here in the States. I will call dad and ask him about them."

"Cat, this is really serious and an open investigation so you know what that means."

"Right. No real information to be given out to civilians. I under-stand. I'll get back to you. Stay safe." She hung up her phone. I listened to the dial tone for just a moment before putting my phone away.

"So what did she say?" Jack was standing in the hallway.

"She's going to get back to me. But she said there are a few European packs that specialize in assassinations. She was going to check with her father." I peeked out the window, and we were stopped somewhere.

"We're sitting in a rest stop."

"I wondered. She said they aren't supposed to be in this country anymore. If he's here on a passport..."

"We can track him. I'll get Washington on that. Dig into our databases and see if you can find anything on Assassin Packs. I was unaware that those even existed." I got right on that while he called Washington. We still had a crime scene to get to.

THE SCENE of the crime was downtown in the non-gaming part of the city. We left most of the shining lights behind as we made our way through the streets. Arriving, for just a moment I felt as though I was on a network television show about parades. Tri-States Developments had a large multi-story building with an attached garage. The short brief we received was that it was a former failed IT company building. At the moment the entire structure and garage were surrounded by marching protesters waving signs.

Multiple roadblocks were at each major intersection. With wide eyes, I stared out at the throngs of people. "Jack, this is going to suck isn't it?"

"Pretty much. I know you don't really pay all that much attention to the news but the Lockpoint pipeline is a major issue right now. Everyone is up in arms. Native tribes, Were Packs, and environmentalists are united against it. Once they complete it, it will reduce oil and gas prices for the entire area. Even though all the parties involved signed off on this thing they are still protesting it."

"They signed off on it?"

"They did. Years ago when it was first proposed. But you know how people can get. Administrations change, land values skyrocket, even the price of fuel and water. Now remember, keep your opinion to yourself and be as professional as possible. The locals are going to resent our involvement as usual."

Each roadblock passed us through until we reached the parking garage. "There is no way that thing is going to fit inside." Jack had his window open talking to the lead police officer. "Pull it around back. The scene is on the first level. There are emergency access doors located there along with the building's loading dock. I'll notify the scene commander to meet you along with the local FBI. Do they know you are coming?"

"They are supposed to. It should be fun." The officer laughed as he pulled out his radio.

There weren't any protesters in the rear, but there were more Agents and reporters. The glares and faces of disgust started before we even exited the RV.

"Who the hell called for you Dalton?" The local Agent didn't even introduce himself first before ripping into us.

"That would be Washington. You know as well as I do that a Were attack means Magical Crimes gets involved. This is my new Probi, Agatha Blackmore. Aggy this is Special Agent in Charge Ernie Valdez."

He stared at me for a moment. "Isn't she a little young for this Jack?"

"She's a graduate of Quantico, top of her class. Agatha is also our very first Witch recruit in the Bureau."

"Is she really?" He nodded his head for a moment. "OK, you can join the investigation."

"Ernie, you know I already have jurisdiction. But thanks."

"You're welcome, Jack. You need our help on this one. Don't lie to me. No way you can control all the protesters and other crap out there."

"I appreciate it, Ernie."

"Just don't put my car on the roof of the building and we'll be even."

I started coughing. Jack looked at Ernie and said. "I don't know what you are talking about."

"Sure you don't. I know you, Jack." He walked away.

I smiled at Jack, and he laughed. "Told you news would spread."

The crime scene was roped off, but it really didn't need to be. Only the police and FBI was allowed on this level of the garage. The body had already been moved, but it was chalked off. He had bled out over an hour before anyone had found him.

"What do the cameras have?" Jack asked the forensic techs to give him the low-down.

"We have the victim entering the garage, but all the lights were out. The recording picked him up calling out and then a scream. The roving security team found him an hour later. His car was still running."

"Anything on the perp?"

"No. The cameras on level two recorded a dark shape running on four feet between the cars. It appears to have jumped off the second level. We found an impact point on the North side."

"Any idea what breed of Were yet?"

"No, not yet. Anastasia has been assigned to this one; she is en route. She is bringing the big rig and her crew."

"Great. That will help a lot. This is Agent Blackmore, my Probi." I shook hands with the Tech and smiled. I would get to see Chuck after all.

"Welcome to the circus Agent Blackmore." He looked at Jack. "We think it might be a bear shifter from the wounds, but you know how that goes. The body is already at the morgue. The locals have agreed to wait for our coroner to arrive before beginning."

"Well, that is one piece of good news at least. Can your people move back for just a moment? Agent Blackmore is a Witch." I smiled again as the tech jerked in surprise. I figure it will be a few years before that stops.

I concentrated on the spell that I wished to use and said a little prayer. Using my Magickal sight, I scanned the crime scene area for anything out of place or unusual.

The air was alive with Magick which was unusual for a parking garage to say the least. I could see three individual spells at work in here. The first I traced to the victim's car. Instead of installing a mechanical self-starter he was using a Magickal one. Part of me was appalled at the waste of Magick on something so trivial. Further examination showed it to be the work of a trained Magick user, not a mercenary. The second spell was a light dampening spell. It was the cause of the lights not working on this level. The third was even more troubling. Dark Magick sparked within the garage. Dark or Black Magick wasn't really evil, nor against the Rules of Magick. It was actually a form of Chaos Magick. The spell was cast upon the walls of the garage itself. They were to absorb the pain and suffering of those that died. They were big spells, bigger than what was needed for a simple death. I came out of my trance with a lurch.

"Jack! Has anyone checked for explosives or some sort of destructive device?"

"Why?"

"Spells have been cast that amplify pain and destruction. One little death will not appease them!" I began scanning the room with my mind searching for something that didn't fit.

Jack ordered the Techs to drop what they were doing start a search of the garage.

"Agent Dalton it's like a cave in here! How the hell are we going to do that?"

I caught the word cave and my head snapped up. Oops. "Hold on a moment. I said a word of power. Ljós."

The garage lights snapped back into existence without warning. The level went from partially lit to full light in a moment.

"Thank you, Agent Blackmore." Jack motioned to the techs to get moving.

"Jack, it was a spell. This could be really bad." He acknowledged me. I started helping the techs look. I glimpsed the local Agent crossing the garage.

"What the hell is going on Jack?"

"Ernie. Did your people look for any explosive devices when they searched?"

The local Agent paled visibly. "Explosives? Here? Why do you suspect them?"

"Agatha detected a spell that amplifies pain and destruction. One small death is not enough for something like that. We think that maybe the killer or killers left something else behind."

It wasn't me that found it but rather one of the techs. Where the first level was devoted to executive parking, the second level was all company vehicles. At the end closest to the main building was a row of maintenance trucks. The tech noticed there were blinking red lights in the rear of not one but three of the vehicles.

"Can we move them?" Jack looked at the local FBI Agents.

"To where? The local bomb squad is coming, but the crowds out there are larger than before. Somehow this is being coordinated. They have to know something is about to happen and are here for it!"

"Ernie the locals and the protests are all your domain, not mine. We are here because of the paranormal aspect of the crime. The spell on the wall further enhances this. If those trucks blow what should we expect? Do you know?"

"None of my people are bomb technicians Jack. We are afraid to even open one of the truck doors to look at the bombs. Those outside hate this company. I would say they want the worst to happen. We are evacuating but without knowing the yield…"

Jack nodded. "Sorry. Get your people out. There is nothing they can do anyway until the bomb squad clears it."

The local Agents, techs, and police began moving vehicles and other assets free of the possible blast zone. Jack and I stood watching them until they left.

"Jack? Are we leaving too?"

"Agatha, is there any way you can shield against the bombs?"

That was a good question. My structured ward should contain the blast if I had the time to surround the trucks with it. But how much time did I even have?

"A ward similar to what I used on those coolers might work, but I don't have time to draw it all out. I could cast a modified one like we have on the RV. It might make it worse though."

"Worse how?"

"I don't know much about bombs other than what was taught at the Academy. The ward could amplify the blast or delay it. I'm just not sure. Do you still want me to try?"

"I do, but it is only voluntary, Agatha. It could blow before you finish." I nodded as he gave me an out. Stroking my bracelet it purred at me again. I made my decision.

"I'm going to try. Please clear the last of the people, including yourself out of here. I don't want to be responsible for their deaths." I reached into my ever-present spell bag and began pulling out herbs and salt.

Deciding that the worst thing that could happen was the garage blowing up, I took a chance. I walked the length of the parking area sprinkling my herb mixture as I walked. Needing to cover the entire line of parked vans I went faster than I usually do. My prayers were at light speed too. Trusting my faith would pull me through, I finished my loop of the line of ten vans. Only half were possibly armed to explode, but I couldn't take a chance and get it wrong. Completing the large oval I sent a prayer to Athena and to Tara to protect both the people outside and me. Trusting in the power of my great-grandmother's bracelet to protect me I centered myself and cast the Ward.

The Ward on the coolers and my lab were structured things that took time and energy to get right. This one was a creation straight out of my head and driven by my intent to protect everyone. It reflected my need and my prayers. It snapped into existence rippling with power. Like waves of heat rising from the hot pavement I could see the spell leeching power from the surroundings. Gazing at it with my Magickal sight, it looked complete. I said a silent thank you to my Goddess and to those that watched over me.

I barely took three steps away before it exploded.

Unknown to any of the FBI, the bombs had been set to cause a ripple effect. It was supposed to be like watching a demolition company in action; each successive explosion weakens the structure until it finally collapses. My shield threw a major monkey wrench into this plan.

The first explosion knocked the feet out from under me. The garage rumbled and shook, then the chain of explosions continued.

Ever wonder what standing on a pile of speakers at a thrash metal concert would be like? Let me tell you. The vibration grew and grew with each explosion. As I lay on the cold concrete, I could feel each explosion as a thump that vibrated my bones. Trembling, I managed to stand. Checking my watch barely a minute had passed. Car alarms and other alarms were echoing inside the garage. Turning, I looked in the direction of the Ward. All ten vans were gone. Completely gone. In their place was a ball of metal as tall as me surrounded by my Ward. Circling it, I could see bits and pieces of the vehicles. My protective energy allowed the explosions to happen but trapped the explosive force inside, shrinking each time as space became available. To me, that was very interesting. I could think of other things a spell like that would be helpful with. Now I just needed to slowly release the energy so the bomb techs could get to the site. I thought a moment and envisioned a balloon. I imagined just a tiny hole to allow the energy to "leak" out and not "pop" my containment spell. I whispered my releasing spell and crossed my fingers. My on-the-fly spells could be iffy. I looked again and saw a very small area of my spell change and watched a moment as the energy began to leak out. It would take awhile for the pressure to equalize, but then I could safely remove the containment spell.

I felt a vibration at my hip and jumped in surprise. So wrapped up in studying the metallic ball I was ignoring my actual duty!

"Hello?"

"Agatha? Thank god! We felt the rumble and heard what sounded like explosions. Are you alright?"

Still watching my Ward ripple I smiled at the phone. "I'm fine Jack. It's safe to come back inside I think."

"Stay where you are. The bomb squad finally made it and are coming in."

"OK. I'll stay right here." I stared at what was left of the bombs and said the word of power to drop the spell. The ball of metal was smoking and rocking just a bit as that which held it in place disappeared.

The Bomb Squad found me a few minutes later sitting on the floor of the garage staring at the mass of melted metal.

"Freeze! Hands where we can see them." I rolled my eyes and continued to stare at the dark spell on the wall. It was very intricate. Someone had used spray paint and covered the wall in a combination of Sanskrit and Anglo-Saxon runes. They spelled out the structure and intent of the spell. I found it quite fascinating that they were invoking Chaos and Janus in the same spell.

I reached into my spell bag and pulled out a small camera. As I raised it up to take a picture a voice yelled at me again.

"I said, Freeze! Drop it, or I'll shoot!" I set the camera down and turned my head. Four men stood behind me. Two were in the typical EOD suits used by most bomb units. The other two dressed as though they had played entirely too many video games. Black suits, black-Molle shoulder gear, and weapons dripped off the officers. Were balaclavas and night vision really necessary for finding bombs?

It was all I could do to not shake my head and laugh. "I'm with the FBI, Agent Blackmore."

"We said down on the ground, or we'll shoot!" Stupidly, on my part, I started to stand, and the officers opened fire. My shield snapped into being surrounding me. Bullets bounced off me and ricocheted into the walls of the garage.

"Really? Didn't they tell you there was an FBI agent in here?" The overly weaponed EOD techs all stood there with their mouths open. One of the men raised his weapon at me again.

"Nope." I waved my hand. The man stood frozen to the floor, his arms immobile, weapon frozen pointing in my direction. "You had your one shot. Now aren't you here for some bombs?"

"Who the hell are you?"

"I did tell you. FBI?" I held up my credentials. Lifting my phone, I called Jack back.

"Jack? You better get in here before I have to freeze some more people!"

"What did they do? We heard shots!"

"One guess."

"Wonderful. Idiots. Is it safe?"

"From bombs? Yes. From idiots? No."

"I'm coming in."

I was watching the locals the entire time I was speaking. "My boss and I are assuming your boss is coming in. Get your stories ready gentlemen."

The second black-clad officer never took his eyes off me as he waved to the other two. The EOD men carefully approached and tried to remove the other officer.

"Believe me when I say that is not going to work. No cover-ups here, please. I am a Federal Agent after all." My personal shield flickered and died. My bracelet gave a slight flutter like it was laughing. I made a mental note to have a conversation with my new decoration.

"What in the hell is going on in here? Jenkins! Why did you shoot at the FBI Agent?" The man yelling was wearing a suit, so that meant he was either an Agent or some sort of higher ranking officer.

"Sir! We approached the subject, and she refused to place her hands on her head and lie on the floor. When she tried to stand we shot at her."

The man was studying me. He looked at his EOD crew and then noticed the frozen man. He shook his head, and I could see his silent muttered phrase. 'Idiots.' I chuckled and earned a fresh glare from the man.

"Did she identify herself?"

Jenkins studied the floor for a moment. "Yes, Sir. She did."

"Before or after you shot at her?"

"Both times, Sir."

Shaking his head, the obviously higher ranking officer looked at his man with disgust. "Didn't you listen to the brief about an FBI Agent being in here with the bomb? I know I heard Agent Dalton's report."

"Sir, procedure is to arrest all occupants first before defusing..."

"Damn it, Jenkins! I know the procedure. Did you check on the bomb in the time you wasted shooting the Fed?"

"No, Sir. Not yet." He looked around the garage.

"What is left of them is inside that big ball. My Ward trapped the explosion as each one detonated. It prevented any shrapnel and debris from escaping the blasts. They went off like a daisy chain. I think the intent was to weaken the supports and collapse the garage. I'm not a structural engineer. I can only tell you what it felt like to me."

The EOD team was staring at the large metal ball sitting in the garage.

"You felt the blasts?"

"Sure. I was standing about where you are right now. The Ward held. That was my only surprise. I will need to remember that one for later."

The officer held out his hand to me. "Captain Reginald Jackson, Ma'am."

Taking his hand, I smiled at him. "Probationary Agent Agatha Blackmore nice to meet you, Captain."

He stepped over to the frozen man and stared at the raised weapon. The officer's finger was on the trigger. "Was he about to shoot?"

"Yes, a second time. I used him as an example to the others. Would you like me to unfreeze him?"

The Captain chuckled. "It would be funnier to leave him like that but his wife, my sister, wouldn't be very happy about that. Go ahead and let him go."

I dropped the spell. Before the man could fire the Captain snatched the weapon out of his hands.

"Max! You idiot. What the hell did you think you were doing?"

"Uh, what. Where's the..." He looked about in surprise. The Captain yanked his brother-in-law over to the corner and had a conversation with both him and officer Jenkins. It involved lots of yelling and cursing from the Captain.

"Are you unhurt Agatha? I would hate to have to explain to your Director that I broke you!"

"I'm fine. The bullets bounced off. Do they really need what might be left of the bomb?"

"They do. Bombs have a signature that can be traced. Type of explosive, detonator, and methodology all go into tracing the origin of the device."

"Well, I can tear the ball apart if they wish. My only question is do they want it here or outside where there is more light?"

"I'll ask when the Captain finishes his discussion with his men. I did warn you about locals."

"You did. Jack let me show you what I found." I led him over to the spray painted spell.

After studying it for a moment, he looked at me. "What does it mean? I recognize the runes but what about the rest?"

"Can you read the runes?"

"Well, no. I can see that they are the ones from Tolkien and my favorite movies. That other scratchy stuff puzzles me."

"Those are Sanskrit. Someone is very diabolical, and they have a sense of humor. Most people would do exactly as you have done and dismiss the runes. They are called Anglo-Saxon runes by-the-way. It has the look of someone just messing around and trying to be cool or scary. Most practitioners avoid mixing and matching cultures and pantheons. It gets too confusing, and they can get into trouble on a spiritual level. Not all the Gods work well with each other."

"You say they mixed and matched?" Jack had a camera in his hand and began taking pictures.

"They did. The alphabet used is one example. They are calling upon both Janus and Chaos at the same time. Chaos is Greek, and Janus is Roman, contrary to popular belief they are not quite the same culture. The runes and phrasing are a bit archaic and strange. I will have to study it further to be sure what it says exactly, but the gist is 'A curse upon your house for attacking and intruding upon sacred and profane ground. May your entire line be attacked and cursed until the last.' There are elements of Egyptian curses along with a bit of Hollywood thrown in for good measure."

Jack studied the wall for a moment. "Is there a curse?"

"There is. But not the kind it speaks of. This spell is designed to draw in and capture the pain, suffering and the life force of those who die from violence. Whoever made this intended for people to die. Lots of people." Now the question remains, who wanted all the death energy?

CHAPTER SIXTEEN

The Bomb Squad didn't like my idea of moving the ball of metal, so I ripped it apart at the far end of the garage. Moving it was the most interesting part. Ten vans at a minimum of five-thousand pounds apiece equaled just under fifty-thousand pounds. That was about how much my new iron ball weighed. Give or take a few thousand pounds. The matter to energy conversion ate up some of the mass, so it was only a tiny bit lighter. I'm not a mathematician or a scientist, but I understand how spells work and how they relate to real world physics. That was one of the funnier things about many scientists reaction to the unveiling of the Paranormal world. We could show them, using math, how magic worked. It scared the living hell out of them!

The only thing that would move something so heavy was not anything available. The techs muttered about forklifts, cranes, and tow-trucks as they measured and examined the ball. After watching them for the better part of an hour, I tapped one on the shoulder.

"Do you want me to move it or tear it apart right here?" I pointed to the crime scene they had taped off, again.

"Move it where? This thing won't fit out the door or even the ramp. We measured it." They waved at the ball.

"I was going to put it over there and rip it apart so you can look for bomb parts." I pointed to the corner of the garage about two-hundred feet away.

"How are you going to get it way over there?"

"Magick of course, how else?" Mental giants here.

"This I have to see!"

I was lying to them about the Magick. I was going to use telekinesis to do it, but I wasn't going to correct them. Very slowly the ball started to roll toward the opposite end of the garage. For anyone that has seen and understood what Yoda was talking about there is no such thing as weight when dealing with the force.

"You guys might want to put some plastic or tarps down before we get there to catch any small parts or stuff."

There was a chorus of 'crap' for a moment as several of the techs ran to get supplies. I slowed the ball down just a bit to allow them to catch up. I could have just picked it up and tossed it over there but where was the fun in that? These guys might all be geeks, but at the moment I was a girl and a hero to them. Why ruin it? They got the tarps down as I finally reached the corner.

"Everyone might want to step back. I'm going to pry the ball apart. Not sure what is inside it or if it's usable." I stood there as they all scurried for cover. A few brought up police riot shields and hid behind them. They wanted to watch.

"OK, here we go," I concentrated on the ball and looked for a crack or dent I could use as a place to put my mental 'pry bar.' I needed to rotate the ball only once to find the right spot.

Using my telekinesis, I pried at the ball. I had to use a ward to brace it, but I heard a faint crack as it started to give. Applying more pressure the crack widened. There was a metallic ripping noise, and the ball split into two almost complete pieces.

"How's that?" The techs ran over and started poking at the two halves with tweezers and small tools. I watched them for a moment and walked back to the RV.

"Did it work?" Jack was sitting in the only non-desk chair eating a sandwich reading.

"It did. The ball split like a melon into two pieces. The techs are all picking at it. I doubt they will find anything in it. There was a lot of pressure inside that Ward when I let it go." I walked over to our kitchenette and started pulling out bread and meat. A sandwich sounded good too.

"So we have at least one Were and a Witch or other Magick user, correct?" I looked over the papers at him.

"That's what I think too. Only a real Magick user could craft that spell. It was a little crude, but effective. The elements were a bit strange. I intend to research it some tonight if I get a chance." I put the sandwich stuff away and pulled out a bowl. When I last stocked the fridge, I got salad stuff for Fergus. It wasn't a fancy restaurant salad, but it had everything in it.

"We have a pow wow with the local FBI and Anastasia is supposed to be here soon." He looked at the clock. "You have about two hours to rest and prepare for it. Remember, don't trust the locals. I'm going to take a nap. Wake me in an hour please." Jack walked past me and went to his room.

I stepped over to the opposite side of the RV and Fergus's barn. Faint music was coming from inside. I opened up the roof just a crack. Fergus lay in a pile of hay in the center of the main room watching cartoon ponies dance around on his phone. "Fergus do you want some dinner?"

"Hey, this is my pony hour! Go away!"

"OK. I suppose I can eat this Italian salad I have here."

"Wait! You made me a salad? Why?"

"I'm just being nice Fergus. No real reason. I promise."

"Ponies can wait, salad is food." The barn door opened with a Mooo sound, and the little Unicorn trotted out. His Mohawk was finally back, and the color had faded out. His purple hair shone brightly again. I still haven't figured out where he got that stuff from. Who makes Unicorn makeup?

"Hey, there's no dressing on this!" He broke me out of my thoughts, and I looked down at him. "I thought this was an Italian salad?"

"What do you want?"

"Did you get creamy Italian? That is my favorite!"

"How about a nice vinaigrette instead?"

"You forgot my salad dressing? It's like eating hay without it! I can't believe I gave up Pony play for this!"

"It's Vinaigrette or nothing. What will it be?"

"Really? No other dressing is in there?" He was starting to whine which he knows I hate.

"No. There isn't. Eat it or wear it. What's it going to be Fergus?"

"Fine. I'll take the vinaigrette. Is it balsamic?" I set the bottle down and stepped off the RV. Unicorns.

"Hey! My dressing!" I slammed the door. He will figure it out. I could hear a heavy sounding engine revving its engine, so I stepped around the RV to see what it was.

"Light on the gas Chuck! Light!"

"That was light." The truck made a loud vroom sound. "That was hard right there. I do know the difference."

"Now this last bit is tricky. Pretend you are parallel parking that hunk of junk you drive, but it's now fifty feet longer. You have to turn the wheel a lot harder and watch the mirrors!"

"Scott this isn't my first time driving the rig! Let me do it please?" The giant truck revved up and started backing into the space between our RV and the bomb squad truck.

"See I can do it!"

"I know, but I have to supervise like this Chuck! You are still only a probationary Agent, and those are the rules."

"You weren't that strict on the drive out here?"

"We were, you just didn't know it." Scott pointed to a hidden camera on the mirror. "Anastasia herself was watching the entire time. You only had to drive on the trip, nothing fancy. This is different. We have others watching us too."

"OK. I can see that. What now?"

"Now? We deploy the truck and set up. This is a biggie. Someone tried to use magic to blow up a garage and assassinated a very important official. Welcome to the big times Chuck."

Chuck jumped out of the truck cab and opened up an electrical panel on the side. He turned on all the switches and watched as the super-slide activated on the trailer. The back began to expand as the computer section opened up as well as the investigation unit. Inside it looked like the insides of a blow-up doll. Things rose from the floor, and others folded down. You wouldn't know it all could pack up so easily unless you witnessed it. Chuck walked the outside of the rig checking the tell tales to be sure it all deployed. He opened another panel and began hitting switches. Auto leveling jacks deployed from the underside and gripped the concrete. The back-up bubble carefully balanced itself. Success.

"All done? Now set up the generators and see if we can tap into the local system. Good work."

Smiling and proud that he was doing a good job, Chuck opened the lower compartments of the rig with his keys. Inside were two, eight-thousand watt generators on wheels. Using his stronger than human muscles he pulled the generators out and fired them up. These were kept in perfect maintenance. The rear compartment held a very long extension cord. It was a joke in the department that if she could get away with it, Anastasia would leave us plugged in back at base and just run enough cord to keep us supplied.

He was heading into the main building when he heard his name being called.

"Chuck!" I wasn't sure he heard me until he turned around.

"Aggy! How's it going? Cat told me I might run into you out here."

"Yeah, this is a real doozy of a case. If you're working, don't let me keep you."

"I just need to find out if we can tap into the electric here." He held up the cord in his hand.

"That I can answer for you. We are tapped in over there." I pointed to the access wall by the loading dock. He examined the wall and took a quick picture.

"I have to check. Since I'm a Probi they have to supervise everything I do." His phone dinged, and he glanced at it. Plugging in was pretty easy.

"What do they have you doing?"

"I drive the truck, deploy the trailer, and get set up. Anastasia has been teaching me about the computer systems and electronic forensics. Did you know she is the one of the best in the world at that?"

"That's pretty cool Chuck. I've been driving the truck too. I really had nothing to worry about Jack is a pretty cool guy. I've been learning so much from him."

"Good. You need someone with skills to help you, Aggy."

"Chuck! Why is the lab on the floor at a twenty-degree angle!"

"That is my master's voice. I need to go Aggy. Catch up with you later." He ran toward the truck. I had to smile, good old Chuck still getting into trouble.

I hopped off the loading dock and entered the RV. Fergus was sound asleep in the middle of his half eaten bowl of salad. Vinaigrette was on the counter, the floor, and all over him, but not the salad. It was all I could do not to laugh as I cleaned it up. Checking my phone, I saw I had time to wake Jack up and catch a short power nap before the meeting.

"Jack? It's time to wake up." I knocked on his door. There was a rustling and then he said he was up. The door opened, and he stepped out.

"I'm going to take a power nap, Jack. Anastasia is here and setting up right behind us."

"Great! We have about an hour so don't oversleep. I'll try to be quiet."

"Thanks." I set my phone alarm and rolled into my bunk passing out.

———

"So how is she doing for real?"

"Far better than all of you thought she would. In fact, she has taught me things I didn't know. You had nothing to worry about."

"Jack you know that we care about you. That's all. The FBI has never had an official Witch before so I, along with Madeleine, was worried for you. Her Magick can be unpredictable at times." Anastasia and Jack were in her private quarters at the rear of the large forensics truck.

"She saved my ass when we had to go Underhill. How is it I don't remember the Fae? As much as I've seen there must have been at least one case concerning them. Right?"

Anastasia folded her hands in front of her face. "There has been Jack. More than a dozen actually. The higher ups know, but you always seem to forget. They instruct my team to sanitize the records each time you forget what happened. Security concerns is what they have always said in the past. I'm happy you remember this time."

"Over a dozen? For real?" He held his head in his hands moaning.

Anastasia let out a held breath. "Every time. What would they do without me?" The words were spoken so quietly that only a Vampire or another Were could have heard it.

"Jack look at me please." He looked up and stared at her.

"Watch my eyes and listen to my voice." She captured his eyes and pushed her thoughts and will into his brain. Only an Elder could do this, if someone caught her, the hidden secrets would be up. But Jack was one of her oldest friends, and she loved him.

"You will only remember what you liked about the visit to the Fae. If something about the experience or what I just said upsets you, you will forget it and only think happy things. Do you understand?"

"I understand. Happy thoughts."

She was about to release him but stopped. He had never remembered the Fae before. "Jack, did anything strange or unusual happen during the trip?"

"One-eyed man. How did the guide turn into the one-eyed man? Why were there giant crows everywhere? Crows and bad things in the snow."

"Jack you will forget everything that harms you. Understand? You will forget the one-eyed man. Forget." She concentrated on his head and slowly wiped the information from his brain.

Shaking his head after a moment Jack smiled and looked at Anastasia. "I zoned out there for a moment. What were we talking about?"

"You were telling me about the fish pond your wife is putting in at your house." Anastasia only half listened to her old friend. All she could think of was the one-eyed man. Why was he interfering on this plane? It had to be the girl, but what did it mean?

CHAPTER SEVENTEEN

"I<small>T'S</small> <small>FROM A WOLF</small>."

"Anastasia, we sort of already knew that. Is there anything else you can tell us about the evidence?"

The Vampire Technician cocked her head to one side and stared at the others in the meeting room. "The hair sample comes from Canis lupus albus. It is a Tundra Wolf."

"That narrows it down a bit. Do we have any Were packs around here?" Jack pulled out his tablet and started pulling up information.

"Jack." Jack either didn't hear her or was ignoring her. I gave him a nudge.

"Jack!"

Startled, he raised his head and looked up at the now mad Vampire. "You weren't listening! I said, Tundra Wolf. They only come from Scandinavian countries or the steppes of Russia. There shouldn't be any around here at all."

"Oh. Are you sure?"

She spread her hands. "As much as I can be. The packs around here are both mixed and singular. Most are local breeds though."

"Damn. OK, I will contact the Alphas I know, and we can start searching." He glanced at me and made a hand motion.

"One of my contacts told me that there is a group of Weres that specialize in assassinations and murder for hire. They aren't local or at least they aren't anymore. The Alphas drove them off. The sort of services they offer are not compatible with American Packs. What that means exactly I'm not sure. I have a call in for more info. When I get it, I will update everyone, but it gives us something to mention to the local leaders. They would know if these Weres are around." I sat back down.

"Thank you, Agent Blackmore. Does the Bomb Squad have anything?"

"We found what we think is a trigger and some trace evidence. We passed everything we have off to your techs to process, but we have chemical traces of triacetone triperoxide. It is better known as TATP. It is the mixture of choice among anarchists and revolutionaries down in Central America. It is used in Belgium and European countries too by the PRC to spread fear."

"Not those idiots? Could they be here in Nevada?" SAC Ernie Valdez stood up to be noticed. We were all in a large meeting auditorium provided by Tri-States Oil.

One of the local police officers raised his hand. "What is the PRC?"

"You might know them better by another name. Many call them the Black Shirts or Skins."

"I thought those were nothing but gangs."

"They started out that way. Today they are organized and lethal. They usually stay out of the US though. They use an organization called the Paranormal Relief Fund to raise money here in the States. Giving up that stream of income would hurt more than help them. I doubt it's them here." Agent Valdez answered my unspoken question as well.

"I've run into the PRC on American soil only once, and it was far from here. The local reservations around here don't want that sort of trouble as most of you already know." Jack looked out at the crowd. "Talk to your informants, mention a new group in town. It might be PRC related, but I doubt it. Explosive labs, especially ones that are making TATP, stick out like a sore thumb. The lab will resemble a Meth cooking lab so be extremely careful. It is made by mixing concentrated hydrogen peroxide with a fuel like acetone or ethanol. A strong Acid is also used in the mix. Any idiot with a recipe and a hot plate can make this stuff. It is extremely unstable and will blow up on its own if the makers are not careful. Look for unexplained explosions during your patrols. In Europe, they mix in black powder and nails or ball bearings for a larger, more destructive explosion. Be very careful. Does anyone have any more questions?"

"Yes, Sir. Is this related to the Pipeline protests?"

"We aren't sure about that yet. If the bombs had gone off, they would have brought the garage and some of the building down with them. Those protesters didn't seem upset about being close to that, so I would say they aren't involved. Many of them don't seem to be the martyr type. The victim's death will most certainly upset the conference. That will be all for now, thank you." Jack turned and began to talk in whispered tones with the local FBI Agents.

Chuck stepped away from the techs and came over to me. "Have you heard back from Cat?"

"Not yet. She's really busy with that serial killer case in Atlanta. I'll call her. I need to see if her father sent her more information about those Packs."

"Tell her you saw me."

"OK, I'll do that." I watched him as he walked back to the others. Being on assignment was good for him.

Jack stepped over to me. "Agatha get whatever you need, we have a meeting with both the tribes and the Packs."

Taking what he said to heart, I ran back to the RV. Not sure what I would need, I started loading my spell bag. Salt and herbs are my standard components, but I grabbed a few candles and my chalk box. I stood in front of Fergus's barn for a moment.

"Fergus? We are going to visit one of the tribal reservations and meet with them. Would you like to go?"

He stuck his head out one of the windows. "Real Indians? That sounds like fun! Where else are you taking me?"

"Well, we have to see some of the Packs out there too."

"Packs? Like Were Packs?"

"Yes."

"I'll stay here. Goodbye." He pulled his head back inside. I had to laugh; he was scared of the Weres.

Stepping out of our camper, I saw Jack in an unmarked Police cruiser. "Hop in. It's a long drive out to the reservation."

"Where did you get this?" The car was pretty nice for a government vehicle.

"It belongs to the local branch. I had to promise not to break it. The meeting is out at the Sugar Mountain reservation. All the protest leaders agreed to meet with us out there."

"Which tribe has that one?"

"None. It's a Pack reservation."

I leaned back in my seat. The Pack Reservations were America's dirty secret of the 1920s. After the Great War and the Unveiling, the Were Packs got the worst treatment of all of us. They couldn't hide what they were from the general public. Responding to fears, the Government created reservations to put the Were Packs on. Like the Native Americans of a century past, they were rounded up, then locked up behind fences and useless paper treaties. They had no choice in the matter.

It took over an hour to reach the Sugar Mountain reservation, all I could see was desert and scrub-covered hills through the car windows.

"Is it all like this?" I waved at the desolation.

"Pretty much. The Packs out here do a bit of farming and some light manufacturing, but there isn't much out here. They didn't get the same sort of deal the Native Americans got. No casinos allowed out here."

"Have you been out here before Jack?"

"Only once before. It was a rogue hunt. I'm not very popular out here. Be careful and watch yourself, Agatha."

The gates proclaimed this a Federal Reservation, but the guard shacks were unoccupied and in ruins. Much of the town was dated and old looking. Even the houses looked like shacks.

"Haven't they updated anything here?"

"Why spend money on useless things is the attitude around here. I asked the same questions last time." He pulled the car up in front of a large meeting hall. Several dozen people milled around the entrance.

"Baby killer! We don't want you here! Go home Fed!"

I stared at Jack with a shocked look. He just shook his head and walked toward the door. I would have to get that story out of him.

Just inside the door was a couple of uniformed men and some suits. "Jack, good to see you again. Still fighting the good fight?" One held out his hand.

Shaking the man's hand, Jack replied. "Nice to see you, John. This is Agent Blackmore; she's my new trainee."

"Agatha, meet John Running Eagle, he's the local Paiute liaison around here."

"Running Eagle? Is that supposed to mean something?" I was not trying to be mean.

He began to laugh. "It's OK Agent Blackmore; I get that all the time. When it was time for my naming ceremony, I did something really dumb on a bet. I jumped off one of the local mountains with a homemade parachute. I was very lucky not to have killed myself. The elders thought they were being funny and told me that I was 'too stupid to fly' hence the running part of my name."

I smiled at him. "Did you ask for them to rename you later?"

"No. While I could do that, I've gotten used to the name, and it lets me meet pretty girls." He smiled back at me causing me to blush.

Jack just shook his head. "Is everyone here yet?"

"They are. Your fan club out there should give you an idea about the reception you are going to get though."

"Might as well get it over with then." He headed toward the double doors ahead. As I got closer, I could hear the angry rumble of loud voices.

As Jack opened the door, the roar got louder. "We don't want you here! Go home!"

"I'm just here to talk!" Half of those in the room were standing and shaking their fists at Jack.

I followed him into the room and downward to the stage. Three half changed Weres, in their warrior form, charged at him as he reached the stairs. I released the spell that was on the tip of my tongue. Everyone in the room froze in mid movement. They were conscious but completely frozen. Only Jack and I could move.

Jack climbed up the stairs and stood in front of what I assumed were the Pack leaders. "This is Agent Blackmore. She is with me. Release them please Agatha."

I hopped up on the stage and dropped the spell. The attacking Weres fell flat on the floor, and the roars of the audience died down.

"I am not here to hunt anyone down this time. I just want to talk. The president of Tri-State Oil was murdered in his parking garage yesterday. We have evidence that it was done by a Tundra Wolf along with a Magick user. We suspect that it may have been a murder for hire performed by one of the Assassin Packs."

Looks of shock crossed the faces of the leaders. Cries of surprise and denial came from the crowd. My eyes narrowed. These people knew something.

One of the leaders of the Pack stood and addressed the crowd. "They are gone. I promise you the Draugr are gone from this place. We would know if they had returned." He turned toward Jack and cursed him.

"Damn you Agent Dalton for bringing that name back here. As if you were not hated enough by my people!"

"I don't understand. Who are the Draugr?" Jack stared at the Elder in surprise.

The Pack leader looked at the others seated on the stage. "I will explain to you and then we are done. Those that bear that name no longer reside among us." He motioned for us to step into the rear of the building. Jack insisted that he, John and the others be included.

"In the wake of the Unveiling, there were many Packs or tribes of Were people. It is your Government that calls us all Packs. That is not what we called ourselves. Pack, pride, flock, murder, and yowl were, but some of the names used." He stopped and gave me a long sniff. He looked at me with an appraising eye.

"This one here should call her family a Pride, but we all are now Packs in the eyes of the Government." Many in the room looked at me now. Both Cat and Chuck had told me it was rare to include a Witch in a Pack.

"We were all pushed into these reservations and had to make an arrangement with each other. The Draugr was a very small tribe. They served a function in our society to keep the Clans in check and conduct warfare. Why fight over land we don't own anymore. We exiled them to the furthest reaches of our allotted land. They didn't stay there. Have you ever fought a loved one possessed by evil Agent Dalton? What do you do when your wife or child attack you in your sleep?" He paused and bowed his head. "They wanted more. They wanted control of our people. We allied ourselves with the other Packs and drove them out. We burned their settlement and banished them. Now you come and remind us of our shame. Why?"

"That is a question I would ask you and your people. Why would they return if you drove them away why attack the pipeline company?"

The Pack leader shook his head. "It will never end. I see that now." He crossed the room and pulled out a map. "This is our territory and here is the pipeline." He pointed out a green area and traced a line through it. "Tri-States came to us and asked to use Pack land for the pipeline. It already crossed the lands of the Paiute and

Shoshone. Money and support were promised to us for the use of the land. It is just desert they said, worthless. The Draugr, curse their name, once occupied this section. We told the man to go ahead and use it. Why not? It was already cursed."

Jack nodded his understanding. "So this section was what was deeded to the Draugr?"

"It was. They are gone. Why should we not make use of it for all the pain they caused?"

"Have there been any attacks or incidents on the reservation lately? Anything?" Jack still stared at the map.

"A small bit of vandalism here at the council building. A break-in. Nothing was taken."

"So they break-in, find out their land is to be torn up and violated by a pipeline. They try to stop it through murder. Did they do anything else?" I looked at the elder. "Did they?"

Jack and the others were watching me. "What is it they did? If we don't know about it, how can we stop it?"

The Pack leader sighed. "Fine." He reached inside his desk and pulled out a file. Tossing it to me, he said. "That is all I have. Take it and leave. Please."

Jack came over and took the file. We all went out the side exit to avoid confrontation. "John, sorry you had to come all this way out here."

"Oh, no Jack, this was a good trip. We have our own boogie men. We call them skinwalkers. Some relation to these Draugr I think. Be careful with this one Jack. Nice to meet you, Agatha, don't let him kill himself."

"What did you do here that they hate you so?"

"Let's get to the car, and I'll tell you." The people from before were still there, but now the word 'murderer' had been scratched into the paint of the car on the doors.

"I see why you didn't want to bring the RV. Is this going to be expensive to fix?"

"No idea. Last time they set the car on fire. I chased a rogue onto the reservation during a case. He had been attacking young girls all over Las Vegas. He had friends here and chose to involve them by hiding out in a barn belonging to them. The Elders denied he was here and wouldn't give me any support. I called in my magical support to smoke him out."

Inside I cringed. I thought I knew where this was headed.

"We sealed the exits of the barn. I pleaded with them to surrender and face trial. A fire inside broke out. There was no escape except through the loft. The rogue took that route along with a hostage I didn't know about. The others inside couldn't get out. By the time I got my support magicians to understand me, it was too late for those inside." He bowed his head and made the sign of the cross.

He slowed the car and gave me a look. "I can still hear their screams at night sometimes Agatha. His friends here were the start of a young Pack. Only the Alpha was strong enough to survive the burns. He committed suicide later. The locals, of course, blamed me and rightfully so. I shouldn't have blocked the doors."

"Jack, he was a criminal. Those kids should have known that!"

"That's the funny part about the whole thing. The hostage told them repeatedly she was kidnapped. They ignored her."

"Then they were just as guilty as your rogue. Forget about it Jack. Where are we going anyway?"

"This is the way to the pipeline construction site. I thought we might look around the former Draugr lands. Maybe you will find something I won't."

"Something I don't understand. If the tribes signed off of the pipeline and the Pack has been paid off, who is protesting?"

"That is one thing I spoke to Ernie Valdez about. A large percentage seem to be paid agitators. Who is paying them is still a mystery. The rest are local college students and environmental activists. They protest just about everything to get attention. The pipeline will actually benefit them. Nevada has pledged three percent of all money made to be earmarked for education including scholarships."

This part of the reservation was even more barren than the rest of the area. A few construction vehicles passed us on the road. They were carrying pipe sections. The road forked to the left, and Jack stopped the car.

"The construction site is down there. According to the tribal map, this road leads to the Draugr town. Or what is left of it."

What is left of it was a good way of putting it. The town was gone. Only one structure remained, and it showed signs of fire damage. It looked as if the oil company fixed it up a little to use it. I could see a cemetery up on one of the hills.

"The plans I saw showed the pipeline coming down this way through those hills continuing South toward Las Vegas. Go ahead and look around. Shout if you find anything." He stepped into the building.

I headed toward the cemetery I saw. My phone rang, surprising me.

"Hello?"

"Aggy? It's Cat."

"Hey, Cat! Catch your serial killer yet?"

"Not yet. I think it's a Were but the others don't want to believe me."

"That is because they would have to call my boss and they would lose jurisdiction over the case. Most locals don't want that at all."

"I can see that. I heard from Dad. The name of the group you are looking for is Draugr. He said they are bad news. They are a blend of Witch and Were. Before the Unveiling they hired themselves out to the highest bidder. On the reservations they were outcasts. Eventually, the Packs cast them out. Dad said he heard they are now based out of Russia somewhere."

"Thank your Dad for me. We know about the Draugr. I'm standing in one of their cemeteries at the moment."

"Agatha, be careful! Dad warned me they were very dangerous."

"I will be OK. I promise."

"I'll hold you to that. I need to get back, but I'll call again. Bye." I put my phone back in my pocket. Looking around, I could see several dozen grave markers and what looked to be rune stones. My bracelet twinged as I approached the stone. Stopping, I rubbed it for a moment and stared at the stones with my Magickal sight. The stones vibrated with Magickal power I could see, spells of death and protection were embedded in the stone. I looked closer at some of the grave markers. Each had a rune carved to trap the souls of the dead. What sort of horror were these people? I backed away carefully.

Jack was coming out of the building talking on the phone as I reached him.

"... Be careful Ernie. That stuff is very volatile. Let me collect Agatha, and we will be there in an hour or so. Thanks. You too." He hung up the phone and gave me a look. "Find anything?"

"Yeah, I did. The cemetery is warded with some sort of curse and death ward. All the graves too. They have runes that keep the soul in the grave with the body. I don't recommend that anyone walk across the threshold of the cemetery. Bad things will happen."

"I'm starting to think this was personal, not political."

"How much do you want to bet the pipeline disturbed some of these people's graveyards? They are pissed, so they came back to take vengeance."

"You know they say that great minds think alike. Either that or I'm rubbing off on you. That was Ernie on the phone. They found the lab."

"Great! You are just a good teacher Jack." I gave him a little push as we walked back to the car.

"You're the first one ever to say that so I guess it must come with age. Let's get out of here."

The ride back was more subdued. Too many questions in this case, but some of them were starting to make sense. My biggest one so far was if they wanted revenge why try to kill innocent people and harness the power?

It turned out the local police found the explosives lab a full day before our meeting. They thought it was a drug lab. Fortunately, they didn't try to burn it like they sometimes did. There were enough explosives inside to level a city block. It was located about three blocks from the garage in the middle of a nice neighborhood.

"Jack! What happened to the car!" Agent Valdez didn't look happy.

"They don't particularly like me up at Sugar Mountain. Send me a bill, and my division will pay it."

"You bet they will pay it! Next time take a taxi! Can you believe this shit? Right in the middle of a neighborhood. Next thing you know, they will be wiring kids to blow up or something. You said you had a lead?"

"Yes, we do. A name too. They call themselves Draugr. That is an old Norse word for ghost or something undead. There used to be a Pack by that name up until shortly after the Unveiling. They occupied a small corner of the reservation. The other Packs rose up and exiled them by force."

"And this is the first we are hearing about it?"

"Local Pack politics are not something the Government gets involved in. They never asked for assistance or help. They just left the area. When the pipeline approached the Sugar Mountain reservation, they told them to go ahead and cut through the old Draugr area. They felt the area was cursed anyway. Agatha and I think this is personal, not political. The Draugr are offended and wish revenge for the disruption of their graves."

"Wonderful. Did the company do the required archaeological survey in that area?" The Agent scratched his head.

"No idea. They're next on my list to visit after this place. What did the bomb squad say?"

"That there was enough here to blow up the neighborhood. They said if it had gone up they would have heard it in Texas."

"Has forensics found anything other than explosives?"

"Not sure. They are in there now so you can ask them." He opened up the yellow tape and passed us through. The house was a two story ranch style house with 4222 Clinton Way, written on the mailbox. It looked like something a big family would own.

We signed into the scene slipping on booties and gloves just in case. I really didn't want to track explosive all over the neighborhood. The front room looked like the living room in every house in America. A couch, a chair, and some coffee tables stood in decorative ways. Anyone looking in either the front window or door would see exactly nothing. The kitchen was an utter disaster. Moldy food and pizza boxes were stacked on every flat space available. The fridge was filled with spoiled milk and bottles of water. Despite the pizza, there were no beer or soda cans anywhere. Only water bottles.

"Whoa! Hold up a minute Agatha!" Chuck stepped in front of us as we headed toward the back of the house.

"What's up Chuck?"

"We found a strange liquid with a mass inside, and the bomb squad is coming back." The men in EOD suits jogged past us and into the back of the house.

"Find anything interesting yet, Chuck?" The big man was looking strangely competent in his forensic uniform.

"We have finished processing the upstairs area. It looks as if there were at least ten different people here, possibly more. In the master bedroom, we found some sort of altar you should check out. We were just starting in on the den and garage when we found more chemicals."

Jack glanced at SAC Valdez. "Anything from the neighbors?"

"No, they chose very well. The one on the left is for sale, and the right is in the middle of an extensive remodel. They have their own smells and loud noises."

"These Draugr aren't dumb." Jack shook his head.

One of the EOD men came up to us. "It's all clear now. You may finish your examination."

"What was it?"

"Someone had filled a barrel with gasoline and melted Styrofoam into it. A lot of Styrofoam. It forms a mass in the liquid. If lit and thrown it has a similar effect as white phosphorus. It sticks to the body and is almost impossible to remove. Very nasty."

We filed into the room seeing the EOD men carrying a large barrel outside. The den opened up to a large backyard filled with empty crates and a bonfire pit. The room itself was a laboratory. To me, it was more interesting than the backyard because I had a real one back at Quantico.

"Do we know how much they made?" I was staring at the open page of a measurement log book.

"At present, we don't."

"Well, you might want to check this out then." With my pencil, I turned the page to an earlier entry. According to the figures and if they were accurate, they made a lot more than what was in those trucks.

We staggered out of the house about an hour later. There were at least ten pissed off Witches and Weres loose in Las Vegas with enough unstable explosives to level two city blocks. Evacuation was completely out of the question. What worried me the most was that they had nothing whatsoever to lose.

"I don't understand Agatha, what does it mean?" We were staring at the Altar that the forensics team found. It was a large one in the smallest bedroom upstairs. Many offerings of food and wine had been made before it. I could feel a certain uncomfortable Magick from the display. A statue of Janus dominated the center. The other half or female half representing the Goddess was not present here.

"Janus is a God of time and change. For some, he is the representation of Chaos. Chaos was one of the Greek gods. It was from him that the others rose to their heights. They don't intend to survive what is coming. I expect they will worship by causing as much Chaos as possible."

"This is Vegas. The whole city is a potential powder keg. We need to narrow it down and do so fast." I pulled out my cell phone and began texting Anastasia.

Jack gave me a questioning look as he drove back to the RV. "We don't have a lot of time, so I'm asking for them to send me all the pictures so I can sort them." My tablet dinged at me.

"That's a pretty good idea."

"Thanks, Jack." I began flipping through the pictures at lightning speed. Suddenly I stopped.

"I may have something, Jack. Take a look at this. What do you see?" He pulled the car over to the side and grabbed the tablet. Like mine, I saw his eyes light up on the object in question. He whipped out his phone. "Valdez? I think we might know. It's the Maximus."

"Are you sure about this Jack? Really sure?"

"Yes. In the crime scene photo's there is a Roman style helmet on the counter in the kitchen. It has a broken strap. Next to it are tools and scraps from a leather repair kit. If it were a souvenir why fix it?"

Las Vegas is known as a mecca of gambling and debauchery. One thing here tops it all in the name of entertainment. The Maximus. Forget football, baseball, basketball, and quidditch. All other sports pale in comparison to the massive games of the Maximus. Gladiatorial combat and chariot racing are what dominates the arena. Blood and sand. Life and death.

CHAPTER EIGHTEEN

THERE IS a slogan that says "What happens in Vegas stays in Vegas." Much of the entire State is that way too. After the Demon War, certain criminal elements moved into the State. There wasn't much here except reservations; both Indian and Were. A few laws were changed, and politicians paid off. Suddenly gambling and prostitution were legal here. But people wanted more, much more. A whole generation now existed that remembered the high of being shot at or chased by demon infused unstoppable warriors. Many liked the adrenaline rush and wanted to feel it again. The racing world got a huge boost from this. Watching cars or bikes race around satisfied some, but not the die hards. They wanted the whole experience. Blood, speed, and death just like their ancestors did. The Circus Maximus was born. Modeled after the original in Rome it was a race track beyond all others. But instead of cars, they decided to use chariots. The original rules were even included. 'Fight in the sand, race in the sand, die in the sand,' became their motto.

"Jack we can't evacuate it. It's impossible. The Maximus is one of those nightmare scenarios that we study at the Academy. How do you evacuate a quarter of a million people? Where would we send them?

You forget that the Maximus is a 24/7 event. There is always some-thing going on inside of it. Always." Valdez ran his fingers through his hair and pulled.

"The helmet proves they have been there. Why else have it? It is the perfect place to have mass chaos."

"Agent Valdez? Does Tri-States Oil have some connection to the Maximus?" I was studying the tourist fliers associated with the sporting arena.

"They might be one of the sponsors. I can check."

Jack looked up from his tablet. "Check if you can. See if the locals will beef up security and try to get permission for the bomb squad to install sensors to look for the chemicals related to this. We have an appointment to meet with the acting President of Tri-States Oil. I'll add the Maximus to the list of questions. Let's get moving."

We climbed back into our graffiti car and headed back toward the RV. So far this has been an eye-opener for me. Witches and Weres working together to kill. I wondered if the Council knew? They almost had to know.

There were fewer crowds on the way back. The police cordon had shrunk a bit. News stories about the death of the Oil Company CEO had leaked. Many of the non-organized protesters were still there, but the paid ones were gone. Jack parked in front of the RV, and we quickly rushed inside. We had killers to find and this meeting needed to be quick.

The main lobby of Tri-States Oil was beautifully decorated in marble and silk. The different textures added a sense of comfort to the surroundings. We presented our badges and were escorted to the proper elevator.

"They are really smooth here." Jack smiled, but glanced above and made his eyebrows bounce. I got the picture. They were watching us. I smiled back at him and snapped my fingers. "We can talk now. They are enjoying some fuzz."

All Jack did was smile and shake his finger at me. Upstairs in the security area, they were cursing my name and his. All of their elevator screens were nothing, but fuzz and static. Nothing worked.

Our elevator stopped at the executive level the top floor. There was the ever-present reception desk along with armed guards. I rubbed my bracelet, but it gave me no hints of immediate danger. A large portrait of the company founder graced one wall. It was draped with a black cloth across the frame. A small plaque hung next to it describing the man's life. It was the first time I heard his name, Benjamin Raines. That was the problem with law enforcement; we objectified the victims too much.

"Agents? Acting President Jeffreys will see you now." We both turned and smiled at the receptionist.

"Thank you." Jack nudged me toward the guards. We followed them to the office on the left. I assumed the one on the right belonged to Raines.

The guard opened the door and allowed us to enter. "Welcome Agents. I'm Acting Company President Cecil Jeffreys."

"Sorry for your loss Mr. Jeffreys. We need to ask you some question."

"I've already told local police and the FBI what I know."

"Yes Sir, I know. We represent the Magical Crimes Division of the FBI. We have jurisdiction over it now." Jack smiled at the man.

"What is it you would like to know?"

"Have there been any Magickal threats or attacks upon the pipeline during construction?"

"Not to my knowledge." He stared at his desk for a moment. "Let me call in Ike McGowen. He's our construction troubleshooter." The Acting President pressed a button on his computer and typed in a message. "He will be here in a moment. Anything else?"

"Yes Sir, Does Tri-States Oil have anything to do with the Maximus?"

"The gladiator races? That Maximus?"

"Yes, Sir." I looked him in the eye.

"Well, we do some of our advertising there. One of our

subsidiaries, Johnstone Industries, builds many of the chariots they use. Why?"

"Those that we believe are connected to the murder are interested in the racetrack. We are just following up." I glanced at Jack.

"Sir, was it the CEO that negotiated the contracts for the pipeline with Sugar Mountain?"

"No, he ran the company and made our executive decisions. I was the negotiator for that part of the deal."

"Then you are the one we need to talk to." Jack pulled out the map of the reservation he got from the elders. "This is a map of the pipeline where it crosses the Sugar Mountain Reservation. Did you send in archaeological teams before building here?" Jack pointed at the map.

The executives smile dropped off his face. "I would need to check our maps to see that exact spot. We contract out our exploration teams."

"This is one of your maps. See the logo at the corner." Jack pointed to the spot. "This document here is from your teams, addressed to the leader of the reservation, explaining why they were NOT sending teams to the area. My question is why didn't they send any? The area was clearly once part of a town. Your own engineers used the only building at the site as an operations center. The town cemetery is right across the street. Why is it the pipeline goes through both a cemetery and what looks from the air to be a place of religious practice?" Jack was all business now.

"The locals signed off on the deal. Nobody lived in that town anymore."

"Did you even attempt to move the graves or contact the former inhabitants?"

"My survey crews assured me we were well outside the graveyard. The ritual area was modern and the locals told us the area had been abandoned. The law is on our side here Agent Dalton."

"What if I told you the former inhabitants were forcibly removed from that land by their neighbors? Technically, it is still their land."

There was a knock at the door. A large beefy man in a skin tight shirt came in. I could see the muscles on him.

"Good. Ike? Have there been any instances of vandalism or attacks on the pipeline? Either now or during construction at Sugar Mountain?"

"Sugar Mountain. That was a real mess. We had vandalism almost every night. Flat tires, spray painted cars, broken windshields, and cut wires plagued all the equipment. Two of our best workers quit working for us; they claimed their dreams were haunted by screams and cries."

Jeffries looked at his man. "I don't remember any reports about that."

"Ben told me not to bother you with it. You were negotiating the next stage at that time."

"Mr. McGowen? Did the crews disturb any of part of the cemetery or the ritual area?"

The big man looked down at the floor and suddenly was very agitated. He didn't want to look at us at all.

"Ike? It's OK. Answer the questions please." Jeffries looked concerned for his friend.

"When we bulldozed beyond the cemetery, we uncovered a mass burial. One of the dozers ran over the top of it and broke through boards covering it."

"A mass grave? How many people were in it?"

"We don't know. I contacted the local Chief, and he said it was left over from the 1800s. Ben told us to fill it in and shift the site a hundred yards to the north."

"I remember that move. I was told it was bedrock that was too hard to blow through. What else, spill it, Ike?"

"When it came time to cut through the ritual site, we plowed it up and buried almost the entire area. I remember looking up at the cliffs, and the whole area was lined with people. When I tried to look closer, they disappeared. I thought I was seeing things."

I jumped in. "Before you filled the pit in, did you document anything or allow the archaeologists to see it?"

McGowen glanced at his boss and nodded. "We took pictures. Ben didn't allow us to call the team in to take a look. He said the locals explained it already. But I had my group document it, anyway."

"May we see the pictures?" Jeffries told him to go get the file.

"I'm sorry Agents. This has caught me totally out of left field. I had no idea." I glanced at Jack and wondered if he was thinking the same as I. The Weres had lied to us.

After a moment Ike came back with a large file box. "Sorry, it took so long. I had it stashed in the secure vault. This documents the entire construction at Sugar Mountain." He pulled out several files and a couple of DVDs.

The acting president opened up one the files and began staring at pictures of half destroyed vehicles and construction machines. "Ike you should have come to me with this a long time ago."

Jack stared at all the paperwork. "May we take this with us?"

The executive wavered a bit. "It is the only copy we have; I'm not sure."

"We can get a warrant if you like. But I'm only taking it as far as your loading dock. That is where we are set up, remember?"

Jefferies nodded and handed Jack the file. "Go ahead and take it then. Please bring it back. They won't be hidden in the future regardless of what happens."

I helped Jack gather up the documents. "Thank you, Mr. Jeffries. If you think of why the Maximus might be associated with your company, let me know."

Ike McGowen's head came up. "The Maximus? What about the Maximus?"

"It might be targeted by the same people that attempted to blow up your building. We don't see a connection between the two."

"Oh. Ben took me to the races a few times. We sat in one of the owners' boxes. Ben told me it belonged to an Uncle of his. All the employees knew him by name, though."

"We will figure it out, thanks. I'll get these back to you." Jack nodded to me and we left the offices. He winked at me as we entered the elevators and I snapped my fingers again. "Are you thinking what I am?"

"That there is a grave filled with Draugr townspeople and the Sugar Mountain Weres are responsible." It really was where my thoughts immediately went.

"That is about it. There may be some clues in here. Have Anastasia dig through it and get back to us." We stepped off the elevator and went around the back of the building to our trucks.

The Bomb squad looked to be gone, but the forensic truck was still running. Gripping the box of files tightly to my chest I knocked on the door to the truck.

"Agatha nice to see you!" Chuck opened the door and smiled at me.

"Hi Chuck, is Anastasia awake?"

"Usually during a big case, she stays up somehow. Anastasia says the truck has a special insulation that blocks the effects of the sun on her body."

"Interesting." I couldn't think of anything that would do that other than stone. Shaking my head, I told myself one mystery at a time. I handed him the box and climbed up the stairs into the large truck. Just like my experiences last year, there were half a dozen techs hard at work inside. Anastasia's desk sat above them so she could supervise and be able to watch what was going on.

"Agatha, nice to see you. Do you have something for me?" She pointed at the box in Chuck's hands.

"I do. The corporate bosses of Tri-States Oil kept records of the vandalism and harassment they received as well as a possible cover-up of mass murder."

"Ooo. Sounds like fun. We will dig into it right away." She motioned for Chuck to bring her the box.

"That box is on loan, but Jack asked if you would make copies of it. We have a working theory, but study this first please."

Anastasia smiled at me and looked at me with ageless eyes. "You have grown a lot since last year Agatha. Are we still friends?"

"I think so. Why would we not be?" I noticed she had a slight tan on her head and neck.

"Forgive my suspicions. We Vampires are all about perception and position. I forget myself sometimes. Ignore it. Tell Jack I will make two copies for him. I assume he wants to send a copy to the archives?"

"Uh, what archives?"

"Ah. He has not told you yet. I cannot say then. Rules are rules as you well know. We will talk later." She looked down into the box and began to read. I took that as a dismissal and left the truck.

Jack was on the phone again as I entered the RV. "... revenge is the goal, or at least that is our interpretation of what they told us. No, Sir. Yes. Yes. Yes, Sir. I understand." He nodded his head and waved at me.

I took a seat by the computer and started to send queries about the Draugr Pack and Sugar Mountain Reservation. I heard Jack hang up his phone and start another call. The information on the screen, while interesting, was not quite what I wanted. The Sugar Mountain Reservation was established in 1923 in the wake of protests and voter revolt over what was called the Paranormal Threat. Political change was ultimately the reason the Weres were locked up. Warren G. Harding agreed to help the Weres assimilate into the population, but his death changed everything. His successor, Calvin Coolidge, wanted a return to normalcy and went against his predecessor. The Weres were interned for their safety and that of the public. They herded entire Packs and clans into towns behind fences and threw away the keys.

"Finding anything?"

"No, not really. Just stuff on the founding of the reservations and Sugar Mountain. Ancient history for the most part. Are there any notes and things from the last time you were there?"

"There are. Click the little star up in the left corner. That tells you there is a Top Secret file associated with this entry."

Peering at the screen, I found what he was talking about. A second window opened proclaiming the file locked and my clearance not high enough to access it. I turned back to Jack, and he had a smile on his face.

"You need to sign the form." He held out a clipboard to me.

"What is this Jack?" The form was self-explanatory. My clearance level was being increased to just above Top Secret, and by signing this form, I agreed to blah blah blah. Why were all these documents so boring? I signed. I lived to learn; this was just one more obstacle to that.

"Good. Let me enter this, and you can read about one of my greatest failures." He sat at the other computer station and began to type. My screen changed color and reset as I watched it.

"Log back in. You'll be asked a few new questions."

And I was. I pulled the screen back up and clicked the star. The screen changed a few times, and the report opened up.

"Jack, did you speak to the people at all the last time?"

"Why do that? I was chasing a fugitive, and after I had caught him, they wanted to hang me. It wasn't my fault those kids were in there with him!"

"Not what I was asking. So you didn't do any background research or interviews with witnesses or survivors?"

"No, I didn't. This division doesn't have to follow all the rules the regular FBI does."

"That I understand Jack, I really do. What I don't, is why there is no background info. What if you came back here again? Like now. How would you know who to talk to? That's why we make the notes."

"Never been the policy for us." Jack was starting to annoy me just a bit.

"Well, it has been the last few cases. I created background files on what we knew and what we didn't for the future to look at."

"You did?" He looked up from the computer.

"I did. It is how I was trained. I might not be the one that comes back here next time. My information will make it easier for the next guy."

"Okay. Whatever."

"So I have your permission to continue?"

"You do."

"Good. I think the Pack we talked to killed the Draugr and made up a story about them being exiled."

He studied me for a moment. "Yes, that is my take on it too. They missed a few, though. Someone was there to do the damage to the pipeline."

"Survivors or descendants are who we are chasing then. I wonder about the timing. Why now?"

Jack nodded. "I agree. Worry about the 'where' for now. We can figure out the 'why' after we catch them. Good work. Double check with Anastasia, see if they came up with anything."

I left the RV and stepped over the big truck. It was getting dark outside. Another day was gone, and we still had to catch these people. The techs were all hard at work as I came in. A video of the mass grave was up on the big screen.

"Agatha, interesting stuff you brought us. Have you seen any of the videos?" Anastasia surprised me by popping up next to me.

"No, I haven't. It looks bad."

"It is. The documentation is the most damning for the company. We have letters from our dead company executive telling them to cover it all up and move to another location. He is also the one that wrote about destroying the ritual area." Images of letters popped up on the smaller screens. "There is a post it note stuck on one of the pages from an I.M. that reads 'he let slip that his uncle wanted something from the site,' do you know who I.M. is?"

"Yes, Ike Mcgowen. He's the man in charge of security for the pipeline. He is also the one that had that entire box stashed away."

"Interesting. Sounds like he was covering his ass to me. This Benjamin Raines sounds like a real winner."

"I don't know. We haven't dug into him yet, but he's next in my eyes. We need to find a connection from the Uncle to the Weres. Jack and I think that our Unsubs are either descendants or survivors of that." I pointed at the pit video.

"We agree. The other DVD was of the vandalism done to the construction site. The early pictures are filled with graffiti saying things such as 'get out' and 'go away.' There were people living here."

"Yes. The Weres at that meeting freaked out when they heard our description of the unsub. It makes me wonder who was involved and who wasn't. But as Jack just told me. Solve the current case. We can come back or tell the locals. Let them chase it."

Anastasia smiled at me. "Yes. Jack can be a good teacher. It's good that you're here with him. He's one of my oldest friends, and I worry about him."

"He has taught me a so much that the Academy glosses over."

"They do that so you can learn it from a mentor on your internship. The program isn't perfect as your friend Catherine is discovering, but it works for those who will excel in it. We cannot repair everyone, so we don't try to."

I perked up a bit. "Is Cat OK?"

"She's fine. I have been watching her. For such a tiny thing she has great power. Chuck is a good match for the two of you. You are the brains, she is the might, and he is the strength. Everything that a good Pack needs to succeed. Go, tell Jack we have this under control." She turned away and leaned over one of the computer techs.

I glanced at the video of the hole again. It was getting hard to figure out, who were the good guys here?

CHAPTER NINETEEN

"Agatha we've got them!" I leaned forward in my chair surprising Fergus suddenly.

"Hey! I'm sleeping here!" The little Unicorn had fallen off my shoulder and was lying on the floor.

"You forget you're indestructible. Go sleep in your barn!"

"How? I'm way down here. A little help, please?" I shook my head as I picked him up. One of these days I'm going to figure out how he jumps up on things.

Jack stood in the doorway watching us. "Ready?"

I grabbed my spell bag and stepped out. "Where are they?"

"Bomb Techs found explosive trace outside the horse trainers area behind the Maximus track. They think they are trapped in that area." He had left the car running.

"Are we getting any support from the local office?"

"Some, they have two SWAT teams on the way as well local support." He had the lights and siren going, and we were cutting through traffic.

"Are they prepared to do this in the dark?" Night had fallen, and only the lights from the casino's lit the sky. The glow from the Maximus was ahead of us.

"They say they can do it. Do you have a light spell that can help?"

A light spell? I thought about that for a moment. I could launch spells into the air like flares that might work better than enchanting the teams themselves. That could go wrong a dozen different ways. I didn't want to have to do the assault with a group of pink chickens in tow.

"I can do flares. It would be too hard to do anything else on the spur of the moment. Mine will last a whole lot longer than the chemical ones."

"I will tell SWAT, it is their decision. Are you alright with going in with them?"

"Of course. They can't be any worse than a Demon. Do we have our body armor?" I had been specially fitted, just before this assignment.

He motioned with his head. "It's in the back. I packed the weapons too. Not sure if you used them."

"I have my pistol, but my Magick is faster than a shotgun any day. Thanks for thinking of me."

"As your instructor, it's what I must do." He passed the main road to the Maximus and drove up to a gate. Two local officers and what looked to be a security man stood guard.

"The road is closed. You need to go back that way." The 'mall cop' didn't bother to ask for ID, he just tried to turn us away. I smiled at the young local police officer that was peering into the car. Having Murderer written on the sides, roof, and hood of the car didn't help.

"We are with the FBI, Magical Crimes Division. Please open the gate." Jack showed them his badge. I flipped mine open as well and held it up.

"They're Feds! What do I do?" The security 'officer' looked to the others for support. My bracelet gave a little shimmer, and I cast the first spell I could think of, freeze.

The two Draugr dressed as police officers froze in place and the security officer, most likely Draugr as well panicked and tried to run. Jack jumped out of the car and held him at gunpoint. "Freeze it."

I giggled at what he said. Freeze indeed.

Jack looked back at me as he handcuffed the fake guard. "What gave them away?"

I nodded my chin at the man he had in custody. "His panic and they didn't look right to me." The bracelet and its secrets were mine and mine alone.

"Good work. It was a trap, and we walked right into it." He pulled out his cell and started dialing.

"So what is your story? Are you a descendant of the Draugr or a survivor of the purge?" The man in the guard's uniform stopped struggling and turned his head toward me in surprise. "Yes. We guessed and have proof that the construction people found."

"They came in the night." I quickly pulled out my phone and hit record.

"Repeat that please."

The man coughed as I sat him up. "They came in the night. We were asleep. It was the night of the dark moon, and our celebrations were over. Dad woke up when he smelled smoke. He grabbed my brother Charles and me, then pushed us out the rear window. He said run! We had a fort in the hills we liked to play in. He told us to go there. He would find us in the morning." A tear ran down his face. "I heard him howl as he attacked the ones burning the house. Mother... we found their bodies in the ruins of our burned house. But it wasn't over. They came back in the morning. They came with bulldozers and men. They leveled the town and buried the bodies. Later, we found others that had survived as well."

"How old were you when it happened? What is your name?" I had him talking, and we needed information badly.

"My name is Michael Odinson. I was eight. Charles was four. We found some others in the hills about our age. The others were from town and a couple of nearby farms. Only one adult survived,

Zacob, the high priest. He said he was asleep at the temple when they came. He was missed."

"Where did you go after it was over?"

"We stayed in the hills and hunted as wolves to remain hidden. The money man found us and told us he would take care of us."

"Who is the money man?" Jack was now standing behind me. The Draugr didn't seem to notice.

"A mundy, but Zacob said he was a friend, so we trusted him. He took us to a place to teach us how the world worked."

"What was the place?"

"A farm. They had horses; it was pretty. It was like a school, but they taught us stuff like guns and swords. I like the swords the best. We got to fight and train. Later they let us fight mundies in the big place. It was fun. We don't die like they do. Zacob came back when we were older and complained to the money man. Something about justice. He took us home."

"Why didn't Zacob go to the police? You could have told someone about the murder of your people."

"Elsbeth tried that." More tears ran down his face.

"Who is Elsbeth? Was she part of your group?" Jack helped the man to sit up straighter and gave him a sip of water.

"She was older, the oldest of us kids. She told Zacob the money man hurt her but he didn't listen. He liked the money man for what he gave him."

"What happened to Elsbeth?"

"She left. Went somewhere else. Zacob got mean after that."

"When you went home, did you mean the town and the fort you built?"

He nodded his head. "Zacob was mad. The money man broke the rules. He dug up the ghosts. Death is the punishment for that. We tried to tell the mundies to go away. That's why we destroyed their machines. But they dug up the dead and demolished the Hov."

I nodded my head, this was starting to make a bit of sense to me.

"Michael, is that what the stones in the center of the graveyard do? It keeps the aptrgangr from rising?"

"It does! Are you one with the faith? The All-father knows all."

"I'm not, but I respect all the Gods. Rest we will talk more." I pulled Jack over to the car.

"How did you get him to talk?"

"I asked if he was a survivor or a descendant. It just came pouring out. Did you catch that last bit?"

"Yes, what is a Hov?"

"Remember when Anastasia said these people were Norse or from the Russian Steppes? The Hov is what the ancient Norse would call their religious meeting places. We only have this man's version since he was a child, but the deaths of his family may have been religious in nature."

"Well, we have the link we wanted between the Oil company and the Were."

"We do. This money man worries me. He must be the one who owned the box at Maximus that McGowen spoke about. But why raise Were children?"

"You are missing something Agatha. They are Weres. They are very hard to kill. They trained them to fight as gladiators. Using Were to fight is against the law by the way. It's considered cheating. But would that stop an owner or partner in the games? We need to find the link. Zacob is the key here. He is the one behind the deaths. Would a high priest know how to cast spells?"

"A Norse one would. Especially if he is old school." I looked over at the gate. "Did you get a hold of anyone?"

"I did. It's my mistake. I got the directions wrong and encountered them first. The teams are set up at the Maximus itself. I told them we would come in from the rear. So we are on our own."

I looked at Jack and shook my head. His lone wolf attitude is going to get him killed one day. He popped the trunk and started pulling on his armor.

"Michael, I'm going to put you in the car now, OK? You should be safe there. Your friends and Zacob can't be allowed to hurt any more people not even bad ones." He barely moved as I lifted him telekinetically and placed him in the car. I stepped around and put my armor on too.

"Jack, I'm going to ward the car. Michael should be safe inside it." We would go in on foot. The barns and other buildings looked to be about a half mile away. I hoped Jack was up for it.

Jack was panting by the time we were halfway there. "Jack are you going to make it?" I whispered at him keeping my voice low.

"I... just need to catch my breath. Let me sit down a moment." Jack sat down on the edge of the road. I squatted down beside him.

"Jack, we can't stay here, it's not safe. What time are they starting their assault?" The sounds of gunfire and a couple of explosions rocked the night. "OK, now it is. Do you need to stay here?"

"No. I'm OK." He staggered to his feet. We could see the back of the stables ahead of us. Flashes from gunfire lit up the front. We left the edge of the road and went cross country to the fence surrounding one of the horse paddocks. Horses were neighing and thrashing about terrified by the noise. I had intended to cut through them but now didn't wish to be trampled.

"If we can make our way around over there, we should be able to link up with the police. Can you contact them and let them know where we are?" Jack nodded pulling out his phone. I debated with myself for just a moment. I didn't want to give myself away, but I needed to do my job still.

My first flare went off behind the barn, lighting it up. The second burst just in front of the barn. Between the two, it was as if there was a giant spotlight shining down from overhead canceling all shadows.

I felt a hand grab my arm. "They said thank you for that. We can go now." He pulled me toward the left. I gently removed his hand from my arm and told him to lead the way. Nobody touches the Witch. Not even Jack.

As we crept around the edge of the paddock, I thought about what Michael had told us. The Draugr Pack was killed for being different, not evil. They were of the heathen faith. It made me wonder who profited the most from the attack and who knew about it. The Weres in that meeting hall were scared, but of what?

Jack stopped suddenly which shook the thoughts from my head. I could see a police officer waving at us from the edge of the barn. Good for us, so we wouldn't get shot accidentally.

"You the FBI Agents?" The man was decked out in black military gear. Our body armor had the letters 'FBI' on it, so I wondered if he realized what he said.

"Yes. Do we know how many are in there?" Jack pointed to the barn.

"Not sure. We've killed at least two already. They have snipers on the roof and keep threatening to blow themselves up. The race-track people say they have a hostage too."

"Do we know who?" I peered around the edge of the building.

"Yes. A big shot named Raines. Claude Raines, but everyone around here called him 'Mr. Money.' He's one of the chief financial backers for the Maximus."

Everything clicked into place. It only left a few unanswered questions. We needed to talk to Zacob and stop this.

"Jack." He was typing on his phone and ignoring me.

"Jack!" His head came up with a questioning look. "We need to talk to them. They have the answers we need to tie everything up."

"Let the teams do their jobs, Agatha! We can finish this."

I shook my head at him. "I'm sorry Jack, you are too old school. We can't just let them die without solving the case. We both know that doesn't serve justice. I'm going to talk to them. My shield will protect me."

"Damn it, Agatha! Can it protect me too? You're still a Probi, I have to go with you." I blew out a breath and sighed. "Fine. But stay behind me if you can. Officer, would you tell them we are going out?"

He thought we were insane but said he would inform them. I glanced up. My flares were slowly dying out. Maybe ten more minutes left on them. Working my way around to the front, I stepped out into the light and immediately drew fire.

My shield snapped into existence around me. Jack was included in the range of the protection. I gave my bracelet a rub.

Bullets bounced off me and ricocheted off to the sides. I murmured an amplification spell and began to speak.

"You can't hurt me so stop shooting." They fired more at me. "I just want to talk. We know what started this. We know how they came in the night and burned the town." The firing died down a small bit.

"I know you were children, but you should have told the authorities. We could have helped."

"You weren't there! You didn't see the hate and the fire they brought with them." The voice came from the roof.

"True I didn't. We know about the graves, and we know how the Oil company wronged you. Let the man go, and we can talk."

"Let him go? Madness! He's the reason for this whole thing! He made them attack us; he tricked us into serving him; he desecrated our dead! He and his nephew destroyed whatever future these kids could have had! No talking!"

"Zacob. Can we talk? I know you tried your best to protect the children. What sort of deal did Raines come to you with?" The firing had stopped from both sides. Everyone was listening.

"I was stupid. He said he would care for the children in exchange for our treasures. I tried to explain to him that it lay inside of our hearts, not in the physical realm, but he insisted I give him things in exchange for protecting the children. I gave him the representations of our gods. They were the most precious things in our community."

"And was he satisfied by that?" I could only image what they looked like.

"For a time. He kept wanting more, so much more. I tried to explain how we brought them from the old world. He told me he would keep the children if I didn't show him the silver mine he claimed we had. There is no mine. We were farmers, not dvergr."

"You took them back from him; though, you saved them. We talked to Michael; he told us what happened."

"I saved them. I brought them home, only he followed us. He sent machines and men to harass us. They destroyed the Hov, destroyed our last home and refuge. He has to pay for what he did. They all have to pay!"

He was losing it. "Zacob! What happened to Elsbeth? We know she tried to stop your revenge."

"No! No more talking!"

"Did you kill her Zacob? Did you kill the oldest survivor?" We could hear other voices and yelling coming from the barn. Suddenly there was a bright flash of light and a tremendous roar. The blast wave threw Jack and me backward. As if in slow motion, the building came apart as someone touched off the explosives.

"Jack! Are you hurt?" He wasn't behind me anymore. I looked around, and burning debris was falling from the sky. He lay about ten feet from me.

Scrambling to my feet, I ran to him. "Jack!"

"Ugh. Ouch. That's going to leave a mark. What happened?"

"Someone blew the charges. The place just exploded."

"I still think my way is better, but did you get the answers you wanted?"

"Most of them. We need to investigate Raines and his uncle some more. If we find the missing religious items we can prove our case."

Jack winced. "Mostly. Give it to Valdez and his boys to worry about. The same with Sugar Mountain. We only do Magickal crime, remember?"

I could see his point, but didn't agree with it. "Come on old man. Let's get you checked out and go find our car. I have two prisoners to unfreeze."

"I forgot about them. We will have someone to prosecute after all." He smiled at me.

I agreed with him but wished there was more we could do for Michael. He and the rest didn't deserve all of this.

CHAPTER TWENTY

THE WORLD RUNS on paperwork and Magickal Crimes is no different. We had to document everything that we did and who we did it to. Plus, I had my own records to update along with our databases. The local FBI branch concluded that there were nine victims of the explosion. We assumed that Claude Raines was one of them. The bodies were burned too much to correctly identify them all. A search of both the Uncle and nephew's properties turned up maps of the area along with mining surveys. The ritual items were sold by the nephew, but he kept records so they might be recoverable. Jack was up to his eyeballs explaining to the press and to his supervisor, what went down that night. It was looking to become this year's big scandal.

Sugar Mountain weighed heavy on my mind. Even though we were turning it all over to the locals to prosecute, I felt like I needed to fix it somehow.

"You can't help everyone, Agatha. Sometimes you have to allow Karma and the law to do its job." Anastasia was the closest thing to a confidant I had here at the moment. Chuck just wouldn't understand. Besides, he had his hands full processing the exploded barn.

"Something is prodding me to fix it. I know I shouldn't, but I have to know. Did an entire town simply burn out their neighbors one night? It will drive me crazy if I don't ask."

"Well, you still have jurisdiction. At least for a short while longer. Go, I will take care of Jack."

I just had to know.

THE ENTRANCE to the town looked the same except for the large black crows standing on the sign proclaiming this Sugar Mountain.

I had called ahead and asked for another town meeting. The elders had balked of course, but I sweet talked them and mentioned that it was all over and that I wanted to inform the town of that.

The same agitators were outside, and they laughed at the car. We had not fixed the paint job yet. They were surprised when Jack didn't get out of the car.

"They are waiting for you inside Agent Blackmore." I turned and smiled at the handsome man.

"What are you doing here John?"

John Running Eagle smiled back at me. "I heard about the meeting. These are our neighbors we trust them. Besides, it's an open meeting." I frowned for a moment. What did he know?

Like before, the room was packed with people of all ages. I walked down the aisle and approached the stage.

"Where is Dalton?" The Chief Elder glared at me from his seat.

"Jack isn't here right now. I called you here not him." I climbed up onto the stage.

"We don't want you here FBI! Go away!" Some in the crowd picked up the chant 'Go away' and began to yell.

"OK let's make something clear. I'm here to talk, and I will be doing that." Several got up from the crowd and approached the stage.

"Sit! Down!" I snapped my fingers, and everyone froze for a brief second. I smiled at the shocked crowd. "I may smell like I come from a WereCat Pack, but I'm not a Were. I'm something else entirely." Balls of flame formed in my hands. "The next person who tries to remove me will get a hot surprise."

"Now you will listen to me. I have a story to tell you, and then I will be gone from your lives. It goes like this. Once upon a time there were two communities, one small and one big. The little town to your North was considered to be outcasts. Believers of a faith not your own. Ring a bell? They farmed the land and raised their children much like you do today. Rumors began to spread about them. They may have come from your elders or from the church. The name of the Pack sounded evil, so maybe they were as well. Stories began to be told about them as you shunned them even more. Then one day the elders announced that they made them leave the area. That the Pack Alphas forced them to go. So a few years later when an oil company approached you about their land you sold it to them. Am I right so far?" I could see nods and agreements in the crowd. The Chief Elder didn't look very happy.

I stepped over to the large TV on the wall and attached a device to it. Still smiling I turned back to the crowd. "How many of you were there when the Draugr Pack was told to leave? Did any of you help them pack or find trucks to move them? How about when the town burned, did you even investigate why it happened?" Several people had questioning looks now.

"Watch this and learn something." I pressed play on the control in my hand, and the TV screen sprang to life with the video that I prepared this morning. It began to play starting with Michael's story.

The Chief Elder came out of his chair at me. "Lies! All of it is lies!" I froze him in place.

"Is it? How about later when the oil company began construction? They found a pit filled with bodies." The screen now showed the pit and pictures of those in it.

"The head of security contacted the elders here and asked what they should do. The response was the bodies were over a hundred years old and to forget about it. So my question to all of you is this. Did you know? Did you as a town and a people knowingly commit genocide?"

Many in the crowd looked horrified and openly discussed it. Others shook their heads denying it even happened.

"We have proof that an outside person of influence paid to have them eliminated. He believed the information given to him from one of you." I pointed to the elders. "That the Draugr were not only farmers but miners. That they had a secret silver mine, they had dug. This man, this human, conspired to get control of the imaginary mine. I say 'imaginary' because that is what the survivors told us."

"There are three left. Only three escaped you and your hatred. This will be investigated. Those that committed this crime will be brought to justice. But not by me. I only investigate Magickal Crimes. The regular FBI is in charge of Genocide. I just wanted to see your faces to try to understand why you would do this. But now I understand that most of you had no idea it even happened." I stepped off the stage. One of the elders grabbed my arm.

"You can't just drop this on us and leave!" He pulled his hand back in alarm after I shocked him.

"No one touches the Witch!" I walked up the aisle and out to my car. John Running Eagle was sitting on the hood.

"You're faster than you look." I heard the 'Caw' of a crow and looked up. Two enormous raven-sized crows sat on the power line. I gave them a sharp look.

"Friends of yours?"

"Who? Them?" He pointed up. I nodded. "Not really. They're pests that love to follow me around."

"Will John remember any of this?" I opened the car door.

"He won't. I just borrowed him for a bit. How did you know?"

"We all have secrets. You owe me, one old man. Keep that in mind." I got into the car and drove off. Why are the gods so interested in what I do?

I was happy I got most of the answers to my questions. More nightmares were something I wished to avoid. There were only a few short months left for my internship. I wondered what the future would hold for me now.

SPECIAL AGENT IN CHARGE

There is something about driving that is both soothing and mind-numbing at the same time. I discovered this as I headed back toward Virginia and Quantico. My name is Agatha Blackmore, and I am a Witch. I'm still a very new agent, but I'm the FBI's first official Witch. That fact alone puts a heavy burden on me. Am I good enough for the service? I spent three years training for this job. I'd like to think during my internship in the field I was able to contribute unique skills.

"Can we sing another round? I'm just starting to get the hang of this song!"

I winced. "NO! No more singing! Do not make me lock you in the bathroom again."

"Why not? It's such a fun song." Fergus my mini-Unicorn and familiar burst into song again.

"99 bottles of root beer on the wall..."

I almost slammed on the brakes of the RV and carried out my threat. By the Gods, if I had to listen to that for another hundred miles? They would have to take me down from that bottle strewn wall. I love Fergus, but his singing leaves much to be desired. I'm starting to think Chuck taught him the song just to irritate me.

My partner and boss, Jack Dalton, usually drives this rig from place to place, but he arranged to take a mini-vacation at his home in Dallas. I hung out in the area for a couple of weeks and managed to find more trouble on my own, but that is a story for another time. Jack hadn't been home for over a year. His wife has more patience than I would have. She just wanted him to herself for a time.

"Agatha, are you sure you can handle the rig? It's a bit ungainly." Jack sat in the passenger seat of the Magical Crimes truck.

"Grandmother taught me to drive with her Land Rover. I spent time learning to handle Chuck's car. Cat was able to teach me the right way to drive, correcting all the errors I was making. Chuck's Riviera may be old, but it drives like a dream."

"A '72 Riviera isn't a class C camper. There is a huge difference between the two." Jack said giving me the eye.

"I know that Jack. I'm not stupid. Gram's Land Rover is a relic, but it drives very similar to this except the steering wheel is on the wrong side. The front half of this is just like a truck, right?"

"It is. This one has a Mercedes body. It was custom built especially for us and uses diesel instead of regular gas. Remember that for fill ups. It weighs around 54,000 pounds empty. With the modifications and our equipment, you really need the extra power provided by the diesel. You have to take wide turns, very wide turns with it. It's a real beast."

I nodded. All spring and summer I had watched as he manhandled the RV around the country. "If I practice, can I drive it?"

Jack pursed his lips and looked in my direction again. "Let's find out. Mustang field isn't all that far from here. The area around the runways and hangars is still paved. We can use that to practice on."

I wasn't allowed to drive until we got to the old airfield. A sign over the entrance read Mustang Field. All the building looked in disrepair and abandoned.

"What is this place?" I peered into one of the hangers as we drove by.

"This was a secondary supply and training field during the '40s for the Demon War. Pilots trained here both during and after the war. This was way before the FAA took over and regulated everything. Today only the National Guard uses it along with hobbyists. The developers keep closing in on it. Soon it will be nothing but houses." He drove us past the hangers to the edge of the runways.

"Switch with me." Jack hopped out of the driver seat and went around to my side. "Do you need to get out?"

I shook my head and hopped over the console and into the driver's seat. After making some minor adjustments, I was ready.

"Now. The main runway is 3500 feet long, so lots of room to drive on. There are aircraft turns every thousand feet so use those to turn with. Take it easy. This rig is a tiny bit top-heavy and will tip over with too sharp a turn." Jack mimed turning too sharply.

"Is that where the dents up on the driver's side roof came from?"

Jack blushed a bit. "It is. I was chasing a rogue and all I had at the time was the rig. I almost had him too. Took a corner too tight and over she went. Lesson learned."

"I wondered. Anything else I should know about driving it?"

"You've driven with me and have seen me follow the breakdown checklist. Too many people forget about the list and rip out the cables or water or even the sewer pipe. The list is there for a reason. Always, and I do mean always, do a walk around before driving off. Before I had it installed on the roof, we used to have a portable uplink unit. I was in a hurry one night and backed right over it. Command made me pay for that one out of my own pocket. Three thousand dollars is a lot of money! So follow the list."

He watched as I made my first turn and lined up for a second one. "You're right. This is a beast to drive." I could feel the entire weight of the rig as we went around the corner.

"Good, you feel it too. Now I want you to make a sudden stop Now!" I slammed on the brakes at forty-five mph, and it felt like the back wheels lifted off the ground. Unlike Gram's little truck, this thing didn't stop right away and actually took more than seventy-five to one-hundred extra feet to stop.

"It's the weight. Keep a wide distance between cars especially on the highway. You cannot stop on a dime without using magic. Remember that, and you will survive this. Gradual stops are the way to go. Leave plenty of room in front. Semi-trucks are worse than this. Including the bigger Class A rigs. Ask your friend Anastasia about hers sometime."

I looked down the runway and had an idea. "Could I use Magick to protect and stop it?"

"I don't know. You are the expert in that. Let's try it. If we tip, you get to right it." Jack double checked his seatbelt.

Pretending it was a chase, I floored the gas pedal, and the RV surged forward. I could see the turn coming up and focused a spell on protecting the RV and making the center-of-gravity shift and bend with motion. In theory, we should be able to keep all four tires on the ground. I released the spell just as I made the turn.

"Whoa..." It was if we were in slow motion. As I turned the wheel, I kept expecting the rig to slide or tip, but nothing happened. We slid around the curve and into the next lane at the top speed of fifty-eight miles-an-hour, which was insane and scientifically impossible. But then Magick was an impossibility too.

"Awesome! Agatha that was incredible. What about stops?" I slammed on the brakes to find out.

At the speed I was going, a sudden stop should have sent any loose objects flying forward and had us slamming into the windscreen. Instead, we stopped, as Jack later said, 'on a dime.' It was indeed awesome.

"Can you leave that spell in place or is it temporary?" Jack released his seatbelt and stepped out to inspect the rig.

I really wasn't sure if it was or not. My randomness has faded some in the months since graduation. Both Cat and I think it's because of my newfound confidence and experience. The training the Council gave me did help some. But Grandmother's training is what helped the most. Something to be said for Traditions. I sent a mental thread out to the ward that my spell created. It was still there and as strong as ever.

"Jack, it may be permanent. I'll make a point to check each day just to be sure. I'll add it to the checklist." I grabbed the clipboard behind the passenger seat and penciled it in.

"Good. You may be ready for the basics. Let's drive some more, passing and parking is next."

We practiced all afternoon and the next day driving the RV. He went over each thing step-by-step including how to 'dump' and rinse out the black water tank. Who knew there was this much involved with RV living? I didn't realize until later that he was preparing me for this drive back.

"I have good news, and I have bad news, Agatha. Which would you like first?" I was at his house in Dallas, and Jack finally looked like he had gotten a good night's sleep.

"How about both at once?" The only bad news I could think of would be the Council of Witches coming after me because of the Dragon I zapped.

"It's not all that bad. Don't worry. I've decided to take a small vacation and stay here with my wife for a month or so." He held up his hands to forestall my comments.

"Let me finish. You have orders to take the rig back to Quantico. Director Mills wants to evaluate your last few assignments. Plus you have told me of your garden. Don't you have to check on it?"

I nodded. The offshoot of The Garden was very important to my future within the FBI. High-quality supplies were hard to find outside of Maine and Mount Untersberg in Germany.

"So the bad news is you get to drive the rig home. I will fly over when my vacation is over and join you." He smiled at me.

"I thought... I mean... Jack, I..." I couldn't speak for a moment.

"You thought your time was up with me, didn't you? Well, it isn't. This is your permanent assignment, full Agent Blackmore. Congratulations. You are no longer a newbie. You still have to answer to me, but you do that anyway. Start packing. According to my calculations, it should take you three to four days of driving."

Smiling, I whipped out my cell phone and ran the distance. "Jack." I pointed at my phone.

He laughed. "Don't believe those things. Yes, it is about a twenty-hour drive straight through. However, this thing doesn't do super long distances well. You will have to stop for fuel at least three times along the way. Driving that long, especially for a newbie is tedious and very annoying. Take the extra time to go slow and enjoy the trip. Okay?"

Looking back over the past couple of days, I could see the value of his extra day theory. If we were pushing to get to a crime scene, that was one thing. I was just headed home. Trying not to go to sleep was the problem plaguing me now. Well, that and a very annoying Unicorn.

"Shall we play a game?" I looked down, and Fergus was in the seat next to me.

"How did you get up here?" I chanced a look behind me. The last place I saw the little terrorist was on the workstation just behind my seat.

"I jumped. So where are we?" He had the almanac open on the seat and was staring at it.

"Between West Virginia and Kentucky. When did you start reading?"

Fergus pranced about with his head in the air. "I'm a Unicorn I can do lots of things."

It was all I could do not to shake my head at him. "Why do you want to know?"

"I want to poop in every state. Can we stop for a rest?"

Why oh why did I even ask him. "Sure, why not. Look (at)on the map and tell me when the next stop is. It should be a little green bed or triangle next to the highway."

"What road are we on?" Fergus trotted across the map stopping on West Virginia.

"Don't worry about the map, there is a sign for one." I pointed out the window. Then I realized he couldn't see over the dashboard or even out the window.

The rest stop was typical of many along this route. Well, paved, lots of parking and a nice tourist information center was the norm. I parked the RV in the truck parking area and scooped up Fergus.

"I will take you outside and let you do your business in a moment. I have my own inside." I placed his struggling form into my ever-present shirt pocket.

After taking care of much needed bodily urges, I tried to find a nice soft patch of grass for my Unicorn to graze in, which made me sound insane.

"Go do whatever. I'll keep an eye out for hawks and cats." I set him down in a large patch of clover.

"Cats! Where!" Fergus looked in all directions at once.

"Nowhere. Just eat and whatever. I really and truly don't want to know."

There was a picnic bench nearby, so I sat and watched him prance around chasing off a couple of bumblebees.

"Those things can sting you, you know."

"My horn is more powerful." He swung his head back and forth shaking it.

Why did I shrink the insane Unicorn? Wasn't there a nice normal one I could have been given? I tried to not look like the crazy owner of a Unicorn.

"What'cha doing?"

Fergus's voice behind me scared me half to death with a fireball instantly forming in my hand. "Yaaaah! How the hell did you get up there?"

Standing on the top of the picnic table, Fergus looked up at me. "I jumped. I'm ready to go now."

Regaining my composure, I nodded. "Sure. Let's go." I scooped him up and headed back to the RV not even thinking about how he got up there in the first place.

Remembering what Jack told me to do, I did my walk around before starting up. The RV looked fine as far as I could tell. I remembered doing the 'clean and fix' spell back at school and thought I might have to do it again before too long. We were looking a bit ragged along the edges. Checking beneath it was last on my list. I looked underneath the front and spotted a shadow that seemed out of place.

"Can't we leave?" Fergus was growing restless.

"No. I have to check something first." I reached into one of the outside compartments and pulled out a flashlight. For Jack or me they would open, but anyone else would find themselves stuck to the side of the rig. Gotta love Magick!

I shined the light under the rig in the direction of the shadow I saw. There was a sudden movement, and I could hear the clicking of nails on the concrete as well as what sounded like horns?

Running around to the other side, I witnessed what looked exactly like a Jackalope scurrying across the parking lot, its horns bouncing as it leaped.

"Did you make more of those things?" Fergus looked up at me from the top of my pocket.

I let out the breath I was holding. "No. I didn't."

AUTHOR NOTES

Wow another book is over and done! Writing this book proves to me that I can write longer fiction consistently. It has been an experience to say the least. My next project is a Young Adult series co-authored with Michael Anderle. It is to be called The Etheric Academy Alpha. It takes place between books 13 and `14 of his Kurtherian Gambit series. Look for it mid to late December 2016. Then I will roll right into Book 3 of The Federal Witch, Special Agent in Charge. Basically we are putting the band back together for 2017. Keep your eyes on the Blog (https://tspaul.blogspot.com/)for announcements and short stories.

I wanted to mention a few things about this Universe I've created for Agatha and Fergus. History is a funny thing. Everyone says you shouldn't repeat the mistakes of the past. So I didn't. As I have written before Agatha's world took a turn in 1915 that changed everything. But what does that mean?

The world changed but no one would know it. Tens of thousands of Vampires died and with them governments and big business. The world took a huge breath as the extent of the damage became known.

Politicians in line for Government positions were gone as were many of their advisers.

In America the Great Depression never happened. Europe was not as devastated as it was in our history. The Demon War was only about Germany. The Empire of Japan is alive and well in Agatha's time. As is the British Empire. Much of the Middle East is still under their rule or advisement. Terrorists as we know them today do not exist in her world. 9/11 never came to pass. Homeland Security is never imagined. Russia as I have already written was devastated paranormally but not politically. The Soviets are still in power but it is much more diluted than in our world.

As our story progresses I will try and fill in some of the blanks and write more.

ALSO BY TS PAUL

Federal Witch

Conjuring Quantico - Now Available in Audio!

Magical Probi - Now Available in Audio!

Special Agent in Charge - Now Available in Audio!

Witness Enchantment

Path to Otherwhere

Night of the Unicorn

Invisible Elder

Blood on the Moon

Child of Darkness

Child of Darkness - The Extra Chapter

A Draft of Dragons

Cat's Night Out, Tails from the Federal Witch - Audio Available

Serpent Con

Darkness Revealed

The Fairy Locket

Witching Hour

The Wild Hunt

Monster Hunter

Jack Dalton Book 1

Jack Dalton Book 2

Jack Dalton Book 3

Jack Dalton Book 4

Jack Dalton Book 5

Jack Dalton Book 6

Athena Lee Chronicles

The Forgotten Engineer

Engineering Murder

Ghost Ships of Terra

Revolutionary

Insurrection

Imperial Subversion

The Martian Inheritance - Audio Now Available

Infiltration

Prelude to War

War to the Knife

Ghosts of Noodlemass Past

Athena Lee Universe

Space Cadets - Coming Soon

Smuggle Life

Double Cross

Politics Equals Death

Cut and Run

A Grand Affair

Short Story Collections

Wilson's War

A Colony of CATT

Unicorns are Short

Borscht is Boring

Box Sets

The Federal Witch: The Collected Works, Book 1

Chronicles of Athena Lee Book 1-3

Chronicles of Athena Lee Book 4-6

Chronicles of Athena Lee Book 7-9 plus the prequel

Athena Lee Chronicles (10 Book Series)

Camilla: The Collected Works

Standalones or Tie-Ins

The Lost Pilot

Uncommon Life

Kutherian Gambit

Alpha Class. The Etheric Academy book 1

Alpha Class - Engineering. The Etheric Academy Book 2

The Etheric Academy (2 Book Series)

Nonfiction

Get That Sh@t Off Your Cover!: The So-Called Miracle Man Speaks Out

Study Guide and Timeline: The Athena Lee Chronicles